VALKYRIE'S VENGEANCE

LOKI'S WOLVES

MELISSA SNARK

NORDIC
LIGHTS
PRESS

ACKNOWLEDGMENTS

Valkyrie's Vengeance is an expanded version of *The Child Thief,* so I'd like to acknowledge the beta readers who provided input on the original story. Many thanks to Carol Braswell, Lucinda Gunnin, Rissa Watkins, and Lara Parker. My thanks also to the individuals who provided more insight along the way: Gabby-Lily Raines, Ana P. Martinez, Pamela Talley, and Jessica Kisia. I can't begin to express my gratitude to Michelle Devon and Lynn Hunter for their patience and shared wisdom over the last couple years as I've developed my Loki's Wolves series. You guys rock!

Sheryl R. Hayes and Lisa Rayns are two of the best critique partners a girl could ask for. Jen Whitten, thank you so much for the constructive feedback!

VALKYRIE'S VENGEANCE

Universe: Loki's Wolves

Series: Ragnarök: Doom of the Gods

ISBN-13: 978-1-942193-05-0 (ebook)

ISBN-13: 978-1-942193-12-8 (paperback)

Cover design by Fantasia Cover Designs.

Contact Information:

Email: admin@nordiclightspress.com

Nordic Lights Press, P.O. Box 1347, Pleasanton, CA 94566

Published in the United States of America.

The author respects trademarks and copyrighted material mentioned in this book by introducing such registered items in italics or with proper capitalization.

This book is a work of fiction. Names, persons, places and incidents are all used fictitiously and are the imagination of the author. Any resemblance to persons, living or dead, events or locales is coincidental and non-intentional, unless otherwise specifically noted.

Love between wolf shifters and hunters is forbidden for good reasons, but Valkyrie Victoria Storm never imagined her star-crossed affair would ignite a war. With the thirty-year alliance between their peoples shattered and hundreds dead, blame falls squarely on her. Forced to atone for her mistakes, she leads her ragtag pack of werewolves to what should be safe haven. Homeless, hungry, and hunted, it's their last hope.

The Hunter King ruins Victoria's plans when he arrives in town. She and her pack should run, but the goddess Freya has other ideas. Children are missing. Victoria is tasked with joining the Hunter—her enemy—to stage a rescue. Working together will either heal the rift between wolf shifters and Hunters or force them to tread separate paths forever.

CHAPTER 1

"Ho-ho-ho-ho-ho! Merry Christmas!"

Cowboy Santa's recorded greeting ended on a nerve-grating crackle. The decoration fell blessedly silent once again. The large red and white inflatable St. Nicholas swayed with the force of the air blower keeping him erect.

Wincing, Victoria Storm started the mental countdown. T-minus thirty until the inflatable doll would once again bellow its holiday cheer. The constant drone of the machine's engine grated on her nerves and hurt her sensitive werewolf hearing. But it didn't annoy her nearly as much as the nails-on-chalkboard static.

She stood at the northwestern corner of a busy four-way light in front of a Western apparel store in downtown Albuquerque. People were out in droves taking advantage of the clear weather to do their Christmas shopping. The morning air was crisp and chilly, but the sun shone bright. Harried mothers herded rambunctious children. Women out for retail therapy moved at a more leisurely pace, chatting as they walked. Couples young and old had arms loaded down with bags and boxes. Traffic moved along at a snail-paced crawl. Vehicles navigated an obstacle course of curbside parking, stop signs and lights, and busy crosswalks.

"Ho-ho-ho-ho-ho! Merry Christmas!" *Crackle.*

"Should we kill it?" Teenage werewolf Jasper shot Victoria a smile and a conspiratorial wink.

"It's just so..." Rotating her head, Victoria tried looking at it sideways. But no, doing so offered no improvement to the aesthetics of the decoration.

"Ugly?" Jasper quipped.

She pressed her lips together to contain the laughter shaking her sides and struggled to inject a note of warning into her voice. "Jasper, please..."

"Hideous?"

She heaved a long-suffering sigh.

"Want me to put it out of its misery?" Grinning, Jasper took a menacing step toward the blowup doll. He hiked his hand, fingers spread to suggest a claw.

"That would be wrong, and you know it." Victoria reprimanded him with a stern frown, unwilling to admit how tempting she found the suggestion.

A month ago, back when she had a lot more freedom and fewer responsibilities, she would've enjoyed a stab 'n run. Before she became Alpha of the Storm Pack following the violent deaths of her parents at the hands of hunters. As their new leader, Victoria was now the center of the spiritual connection shared by all the members. Today, her conscience dinged her for even daring to consider it. A proper leader didn't engage in vandalism or juvenile pranks.

"Blowup Santa dolls are wrong."

"Jasper..." Exasperation edged her voice. Her struggle to not dissolve into giggles hurt. "I said no."

"Huh." As Jasper huffed, his long arms swung far and wide. He came within inches of striking one of the many pedestrians crowding the sidewalks. The woman performed a sharp swerve to avoid getting hit and shot him a nasty glare as she passed.

"But I'm bored. How much longer do we have to wait?"

Victoria ducked and slipped neatly under his waving arm. The fifteen-year-old's hands and feet were larger than the rest of his body, making his movements awkward.

At a couple inches shy of five feet, the top of her head was even with his mid-chest. She had the muscular build of a dancer. Even though it had been years since her last formal training, she moved with the grace and precision of a ballerina.

"I don't know for certain," she said. "Freya didn't provide any specifics."

"But it has to be right here on this exact corner?" He stabbed at the ground and then flung his arm toward the opposite street corner. "Why can't it be over there?"

She settled her hands on her hips. "What, are you four? The goddess has commanded that we wait right here, so this is where we wait."

"But jeez, we've been here over an hour now." He stared at the invisible watch on his wrist and pulled the estimate out of thin air.

"It's been twenty minutes at most. How long we've been here is beside the point," she explained. "When a goddess tells you to wait–"

"You wait."

She nodded. "We wait."

Jasper didn't miss a beat. "Just what are we waiting for?"

"Freya didn't say."

His tongue poked between his teeth and past his lips. "Can't you ask?"

"One does not interrogate a goddess." Victoria frowned over his impertinence. All the while, she acknowledged her own edginess, feeling very much the hypocrite. Mentally, she extended a prayer to Freya. *Goddess, what are we waiting for?*

Freya's gossamer giggle flittered through her mind. *Who is the child now?*

Victoria sighed and replied telepathically, *Well played.*

Just a little longer, my priestess. Be patient, please.

I'm trying, but Jasper's not making it easy.

"I'm bored." Jasper paced furiously. "I mean, like, *really* bored."

Victoria bit her tongue. Through the pack bond, she felt Jasper's impatience as if it were her own emotion. As pack mates, they shared an enduring and mystical connection. The empathic and spiritual union served as the foundation of their magic and held their social group together. It was most effective at close range. Only extreme trauma provided enough potency to unify them across great distances.

Glancing around, she resisted the desire to nag further. At twenty-four, she was nine years older than the boy, but it often felt like much more. She wondered how he'd reduced her to acting like his mother.

Her grungy appearance didn't help her disposition. She wore her pale blonde hair back in a braid. It had been weeks since she'd indulged in luxuries like makeup or nice clothing. Hot meals were few and far between, hot showers were even rarer.

"Did Freya hint at why we're here?" Jasper asked. "Are you a priestess or a Valkyrie?"

"Good question." She rocked on her heels, surprised at the boy's ability to parse the two. Her duties as Freya's priestess and Odin's Valkyrie often proved compatible. But the two things were far from the same. Not everyone understood that, even within her own pack.

"If you're here as a Valkyrie, I'll finally get to see you collect the souls of slain warriors destined for Valhalla." Eagerness energized the boy's voice, making it clear which option he preferred.

"It seems unlikely this will be the location of a great battle." She cast her gaze about the bustling venue. Not a warrior in sight. "You wouldn't be able to see the spirits of the fallen anyway."

"How do you know who to take?" He leaned forward, a bloodthirsty gleam in his eyes. Like most young men, Jasper loved stories of valor and glory, the gorier the better.

She smiled, willing to indulge him. Anything to alleviate his boredom and her own. "A Valkyrie witnesses the warrior's death with her own two eyes. If she finds the man or woman worthy, then the soul is collected and escorted to Valhalla to serve in Odin's army."

"Across Bifröst." Jasper's eyes gleamed.

She nodded. "Yes, across the Rainbow Bridge."

"That's something I can't wait to see."

Her smile lapsed and her eyebrows knit, creasing her forehead. "Don't be too eager. You won't cross Bifröst until you've died. Goddess willing, that won't be for a very long time."

Jasper hauled up, crossing his arms. A mutinous scowl etched the lines of his face. "Once I die, I'll be with my mother and father again."

Victoria's concern morphed into horrified realization. "Jasper, *no*. Your mom and dad died defending the pack. They fought so you could live. Your duty is to honor their sacrifice. To do so, you must live, grow old enough to become a man and take a mate, and have children of your own. That is how we commemorate those who have passed."

Grief pressed upon her, an awful pressure within. She had no relief. Not even tears. Her conscience refused to permit the self-indulgence. As Alpha, she couldn't afford to show weakness. Not while the others looked to her for strength.

Jasper stared at her in guilty silence and then averted his gaze. His mouth turned down in a pout. "I'm starving."

"I know." Victoria squeezed two fingers into the front pocket of her skintight jeans and fished out a crumpled twenty. Gnawing her lower lip, she stared at the last of her cash. She loathed parting with it. Especially since she couldn't risk accessing her bank accounts or credit cards.

Not with hunters after her and her pack.

Her stomach rumbled its emptiness, a noisy reminder she hadn't eaten in two days. As the Alpha wolf, Victoria had a duty to see to it all her pack mates ate properly and regularly, an area where she'd failed shamefully. The well-being of the pack's youngest members took priority. Even if it meant the adults spent long nights dining on squirrels and gophers at the park.

She forked the money over to him. "Here. Take this and go get something to eat."

He caught the bill in one greedy hand. He glanced down, and proclaimed, "Thanks!" He took off like a shot down the sidewalk. If it weren't for the fact he was running on pavement, he'd have raised a cloud of dust in his wake.

Turning so she could follow his progress, Victoria watched him uneasily. Allowing the teenager out of her sight wasn't an easy thing to do. It took all her self-control not to chase after him like an overprotective hen. She managed to remain outwardly calm, but a flight of moths banged around inside her gut. Still, she couldn't treat him like a pup. Jasper was a young male werewolf intent on asserting his independence and proving himself. His testosterone exceeded his common sense by an exponential factor. At best she managed his stupider impulses and hoped he didn't figure it out.

Being stuck out in the open, surrounded by normal humans, agitated her primal instincts. As a werewolf, she radiated a predatory aura. People shied away from her and circled to either side to avoid coming too close.

Hunters, however, were a whole nother matter. Superior numbers and resources gave them an advantage. Since they were human, they blended into crowds. She could be under observation, unaware of the danger until it was too late.

Shifting her stance, she scanned the passing faces, ever watchful. Her imagination cultivated suspicion, perceiving potential enemies everywhere. Being the hunted instead of the hunter was exhausting, and she despised it. Werewolves were top predators, not prey animals.

Freya's voice spilled through Victoria's mind. *I'm sorry for placing you and your pack mates in the path of danger, Victoria. Please believe me. It is necessary for you to be here.*

Her lips parted, and she expelled her breath. *I know, Goddess. No apologies are necessary. I'm simply tired...*

I am trying to locate a safe haven for your pack, but our options are limited. Perhaps if you reconsidered the possibility of taking a mate...

Victoria cringed. Two weeks ago, her lover, Daniel Barrett, was murdered right in front of her. She had failed to protect him and wasn't able to heal his grievous injuries. His loss eviscerated her, leaving an aching hole in her chest and her life.

She gulped air. *My Lady, please. I know it'd be the prac-*

tical thing to do, but I can't—not yet. Right now I can't even think about another man.

Freya's voice softened. *I don't mean to be insensitive or cruel.*

I know that too.

In the distance, Victoria spotted Jasper's tall, slim form as he emerged from a corner deli, carrying a white paper bag. She breathed a sigh of relief to have him back in her line of sight. As he walked toward her, she turned her head and tried to look like she wasn't watching him.

You're being far too obvious. More to the right, Freya advised.

Mouth twisted in a grimace, Victoria spun on her toes and almost walked through the restless spirit of a woman. An icy hand closed around her arm. Startled, she rocked on her heels and wind-milled her arms to avoid tipping over. The chill of the grave swept through her body. Gasping, she froze, staring at the distraught apparition. Without question, *this* was why Freya had commanded her to wait.

"The child thief has stolen my son! Help me. Please!" The woman had light brown hair and an olive-toned complexion. A white nightshirt, stained with dried blood, hung to mid-thigh above her bare legs and feet. Her appearance mirrored the condition of her body at the time of death. Dark bruises marred her face and throat, and she had defensive wounds on her hands and fore-arms. The side of her skull had been bashed in.

"Please, Michael is all alone. He's so scared. I need you," the spirit pleaded, taking advantage of Victoria's silence.

Her gut clenched. As Valkyrie and priestess, Victoria had a duty to respond to a spirit's call for help. As a nurse, a healer, she had a nurturing nature and rarely passed on an opportunity to render assistance to those in need. The circumstances left her questioning Freya's wisdom, even though such thoughts were wrong. With resources so scarce and her pack's straits so dire, she wasn't sure she could take the risk. Living people were counting on her.

"I'm sorry," she said, "but I don't think I can help you."

"You must help me," the woman pleaded. "No one can see or hear me."

"Do you understand why that is?"

Approaching at a jaunty trot, Jasper skidded to a halt. His bright eyes focused on the empty spot before her, and his eyebrows rose, disappearing beneath his lank brown bangs. His tongue flickered across his lips and moistened them against the aridness of the winter air.

"What's up?" he asked, eyes bright with curiosity. "Is a ghost here?"

"Shhh." Victoria waved a silencing hand at him. She cast an anxious glance about, concerned their odd behavior would attract the wrong sort of attention.

Neither Jasper nor any of the other humans present could see the dead woman. They lacked Victoria's gift of spirit sight.

Fortunately, no one spared them a second glance.

Ignoring her shushing, Jasper bounced on the balls of his feet. "What does it want? C'mon, tell me what's going on!"

Victoria stepped closer to him and dropped her voice. "It's a woman. She says her son was kidnapped, and she needs me to help him."

Jasper grinned. "Cool!"

"Not so much for her." Victoria glared at him, irritated with the teen's insensitivity. Not that she really blamed the boy for craving excitement, but their lives were already dangerous enough. They didn't need to add to it.

"Find out what we can do for her," Jasper urged. He had a good nature and a kind heart, but he didn't take the dangers the pack faced into account. He failed to consider how assisting the ghost would sap their resources and expose them to discovery.

Rolling her eyes, Victoria exhaled through her nostrils so her breath formed a cloud of vapor on the brisk air. Born and raised in Arizona, she found the extreme winter temperatures of the high desert familiar. The thin air left her lightheaded.

"Come over here so we can speak privately," Victoria

said, addressing both the spirit and the boy. She shook off the ghost's hand.

Victoria grasped Jasper's forearm and moved out of the path of pedestrians. The fifteen-year-old stood a full head taller than her and outweighed her by a whole lot, but she moved him with ease. He lacked the stature of an adult male and deferred to her because she outranked him within their pack's hierarchy. They sought shelter in the natural alcove provided by the Western apparel storefront.

The dead woman followed.

"I'm sorry, but I don't know how I can help you," Victoria said. "I have to protect my own people."

The spirit moaned, low and anguished.

Jasper cut in, "Victoria, we have to help her! It's the right thing to do."

Victoria stifled a groan. *Yep. Too much testosterone, no common sense.*

The ghost mother clasped her hands together as if praying. "Please, he's going to be eaten."

Horrified, Victoria flinched, and her reluctance crumbled. It was better to die than dishonor her calling. "Where's Michael at now?"

The woman opened her mouth as if to offer a ready answer, but her face froze in an expression of anguish. "I... I... don't know. He's close, and it's so dark. Please, he's so scared."

Victoria's nostrils flared. What was it with ghosts? Never capable of providing straight, simple answers. "I'll need more than that to help him," she said, swallowing her impatience. "If only you can give me some way to find him."

"I-I don't know." The outline of the spirit's body wavered.

Victoria's sense of urgency spiked. Afraid the distressed ghost would dissipate, she softened her tone. "What's your son's full name?"

The woman's flickering form steadied. "Michael," she said. "Michael Allen Frasier."

"Good, that'll help me find Michael," Victoria said. "What's your name?"

The spirit blinked. "June," she answered with less conviction. "June Frasier. I'm thirty-two. I'm a court reporter."

Victoria nodded, hoping the gestures would encourage the spirit. The conversation was progressing better. The woman had volunteered more than she'd asked. "How old is Michael?"

June's lips quivered, and her eyes filled with tears. She grabbed Victoria's hand. "He's six. Please, you have to find him. He's all alone, and he's so scared."

"Okay, tell me where he is, and I'll look for him." Victoria glanced up and down the busy street. Her wary gaze watched to see if their odd behavior was attracting attention. Fortunately, none of the shoppers appeared to have noticed.

June's eyes widened. She shoved a fist into her mouth and bit her knuckles. Static ran through her pattern so she flickered, indicating she might wink out at any moment.

Ghosts were displaced souls trapped between the planes of existence. Their ability to interact with the physical realm depended on many factors. Force of personality played an instrumental role, as did the trauma associated with a person's death. Because June lacked a solid presence, Victoria suspected the only thing anchoring the mother was her love for her son.

"Where did you die?" Victoria's sense of urgency increased with each passing second. "Is your child still near your body?"

"What do you mean? I'm not dead!" June stared at her in open horror.

"No, wait! Don't go!" Victoria lunged, grabbing for the ghost, but her hand passed through the spirit's arm. Within seconds, June had dissolved into a shower of gray and white sparkles.

"Damn it!" Victoria stomped her foot on the pavement.

"What happened?" Jasper asked, dancing with excitement.

"She's gone." Victoria ran a hand across her scalp to the base of her braid.

"Gone? Where'd she go?"

Victoria exhaled a breath she'd been holding. "I don't know. Sometimes the soul crosses over once the person realizes they're dead. Other times, too much stress can disrupt the ghost for a while. She might recover and come back."

Jasper's fists clenched. "How long will that take? We can't wait! If her son's been taken, he needs help right away."

"We know their names. There are other ways of finding them." Reaching out psychically, she sent a wave of cooling energy over Jasper, soothing his wolf.

The boy's rigid stance relaxed somewhat, but his tone remained anxious. "Where will we start?"

Victoria opened her mouth but froze before an answer crossed her lips. Her gaze locked on the classic muscle car parked alongside the curb on the other side of the street, a few hundred feet down.

Her breath hitched. Was that...? Could it be...?

"Hey, Victoria? What's wrong? What're you looking at?" Jasper's voice buzzed in her ears, increasingly insistent. The meaning of his words failed to register.

Heart in her throat, she walked north. Pedestrians passed her on either side, but she barely noticed them. Before she got close enough to read the Arizona plates below the rear bumper, she verified her suspicions. The 1970 Chevelle SS 454 convertible was red with black racing stripes and a buttery soft white leather interior. With as much time as she'd spent in the car with her lover, she'd know it anywhere.

It had belonged to Daniel.

CHAPTER 2

The nearer Victoria got to the car, the louder her heart thundered in her ears and slammed against her breastbone. The top was down, and the raised hood concealed the identity of the man leaning over the engine. Only long denim clad legs and scruffy black short boots were visible. He wore a revolver strapped to his thigh.

Vertigo spun the world, worsening the lightheadedness from the altitude. Maybe she was breathing too fast or not at all. She lost all sense of connection with her own body.

The first time Daniel took her out on a "date," it had been under the pretext of a vampire hunt. Working in tandem, wolf and hunter slayed an entire nest, and the only difficulty they encountered happened on the way home. The Chevelle had overheated on a dirt road in the middle of the desert, miles from anywhere. When the temperature indicator climbed into the danger zone, he pulled off to the dirt shoulder. "We need to stop for a while."

"You've got to be kidding." The convertible's top was down, so Victoria tilted her head and let her long hair tumble down her back. She stared up at the clear, starry sky and then shot him a challenging grin. "This has got to be the most tired ploy in the book for getting a girl alone."

He turned off the engine and released his seatbelt. His white teeth gleamed in a cocky smirk. "It's not a ploy."

"Oh, it isn't?"

"No, I'd never risk damaging the engine like that."

Her eyes narrowed. She flushed with mixed irritation and embarrassment. Okay, so maybe her assumption was a bit conceited. Her ego certainly stung. In her defense, the man couldn't exactly mask his attraction from her sensitive nose. His basal aroma was warm and earthy, thick with arousal, distinctively male and virile.

Her lips thinned. What the hell was she doing out here alone with him anyway? Hunters were off-limits, not to mention completely inappropriate.

She noticed he hadn't taken out his cell phone or made any attempt to get out of the car. She promoted him, tone impatient. "Are you calling for a tow truck?"

"There's no service out here." He smiled. "Maybe in a bit. Let's just give it a chance to cool down first."

"Maybe I'll shift and run home." Punching the release button on her seatbelt, she snapped the safety strap aside. She bunched her legs beneath her, intending to boost herself over the front door. "I'll let a tow truck know where to find you."

"Victoria." Daniel caught her forearm in a firm grip.

Her head swiveled, and she stared at his hand. "Be careful you don't lose that."

"I think I'll take my chances." Drawing her toward him, he captured her gaze. His pupils were fully dilated. He never flinched or wavered. He radiated unshakable confidence. His strong shoulders framed a rock solid stance. Passionate red-toned hues dominated his aura.

"You're a brave man." From beneath lowered lashes, she looked up at him. She gripped his forearm, pressing hard enough with her nails to leave half-moon indentations. She found him appealing, but she'd be damned if she'd make it easy for him.

"I don't need to play games. I know what I want," Daniel said in a tone strong with conviction. He leaned in close so the heat of his breath caressed her lips.

"Are you sure? *This* is against the rules." Over their locked arms, she dared him with her smile, invited him with the breathy rasp of her voice.

"Fuck the rules."

"Oh, really?" Her snicker conveyed skepticism. "I'm sorry. Are you *not* Jake Barrett's oldest son who does everything his daddy says?"

His brown eyes glittered with anger, and his jaw tightened. His dangerous chuckle sent shivers coursing through her. "Not everything."

The roomy front seat of the Chevelle suddenly seemed cramped, and the man loomed larger than life. He oozed raw charisma. Wolf shifters had higher basal body temperatures than humans, but she perceived him as toasty warm. His soul radiated intense heat that caressed her skin like sunlight.

"No?" Victoria arched her eyebrows. Her hand settled on the base of his throat, her fingertip pressed to the jugular notch, monitoring his strong pulse.

"No." He exhaled.

She breathed in, learning his scent, hungry to experience his essence. She broke eye contact to stare at his defined mouth and dragged the tip of her tongue across her upper lip in a deliberate tease. "Prove it," she dared. "Show me."

He leaned in close enough so her hand became trapped between them. His lips ghosted across hers, soft and silken. He was rich and smoky on her tongue, molten heat, a unique flavor she fancifully likened to cardamom soaked in burgundy.

She hadn't held him, touched him, or tasted him in

weeks, and she never would again. Recoiling from the bittersweet memory, Victoria forced her thoughts back to the present. Daydreams were an indulgence she couldn't afford.

The man bent over the Chevelle's engine straightened, and his top half emerged from beneath the raised hood. She stared, expecting to see Daniel, and for a full second her imagination supplied the memory she desired. He stood before her, all six-foot-plus of him, handsome and healthy, bursting with vitality.

Quintessentially alive.

Except, in simple reality it couldn't be him. That would be impossible. She'd witnessed Daniel's death with her own two eyes. The vision was a lie, an illusion embodying her heart's desire. She blinked and reality asserted itself.

Fear coursed through her body, chilling her blood to a toxic sludge.

Daniel's father stood on the opposite side of the street. Jake Barrett, the notorious Hunter King, the man responsible for the death of her parents and most of her pack, and a living legend in his own right. Men revered him, monsters feared him. Lots of things were said about him, often impolite, but all were in agreement on one basic point—the man was a scary, seemingly invincible badass.

Jake stared at her in clear surprise. Squaring his broad

shoulders, he adopted a wide set stance. At six-foot plus, he had a dense, muscular physique. Salt-and-pepper dappled his brown hair. Sixty years of exposure to the desert sun had weathered his skin to tanned leather. Battle scars marred his flesh. She knew a dagger tattoo covered the back of his left forearm even though she didn't have a clear view of it from her current position. According to stories, the tattoo became a physical weapon in his hand. A knife with a blade that glowed like molten steel and seared everything it touched.

Time stopped. Reality narrowed to a microcosm. Only wolf and hunter existed. She cringed, recoiling from the accusation in Jake Barrett's eyes. A serpent coiled within her chest, constricting her lungs and crushing her heart. Outside their private bubble, the real world continued to turn. People strolled past on the side-walks. Voices and engines combined to form a muted hum. Cars crammed the street between them.

Blinking, Victoria tried to force her rigid body to relax. She extended her thoughts to Freya. *Goddess, he seems as surprised to see me as I am to see him. This can't be a coincidence that he's here in Albuquerque, on the same street, at the exact time that I am.*

A hesitation preceded Freya's answer, and then she spoke in a voice laden with remorse. *I'm sorry, Victoria. It was vitally important that he find you. You'll need his help to save the little boy.*

Shocked at the betrayal, Victoria spoke aloud, "Goddess, what have you done? He's more likely to kill me and the members of my pack than to help!"

Beside her, trembling Jasper latched onto her elbow. "V-Victory, is that?"

"It's okay. Don't panic." Her hand closed on the teenager's forearm, delivering a reassuring squeeze. Through the pack bond, she pushed the command to his beast. Her first and foremost instinct as Alpha was to protect the younger wolf.

The Hunter King's unwavering gaze appraised her and then Jasper in turn. In a useless but reflexive gesture, Victoria stepped in front of the boy. Despite the background din, the hunter conveyed the scary impression of knowing what they were saying.

"Calm?" Jasper's voice soared toward soprano. "But you just said he was going to kill us!"

She winced. "I misspoke. If he wanted us dead, we'd already be dead."

"Th-th-that's hardly reassuring!"

Jake Barrett's head tilted, and his brow lifted in a silent question.

She glanced down the street in the indicated direction toward a pedestrian crosswalk. The stoplight stood in front of the Western apparel store with the blowup Cowboy Santa. Turning, she met his gaze again and nodded her agreement.

When he walked toward the crosswalk, the dreadful knot in her gut hardened to an aching agony. She should run, but she couldn't. Victoria always struggled with blind obedience to her mistress. Freya's will trumped hers, and the goddess had made her desires known. This confrontation needed to happen whether Victoria wanted it or not.

In answer to her doubts, Freya touched her mind. *Have faith, Victoria. I am acting in our best interests.*

Yes, Goddess. Victoria twisted to the teenager. "Jasper, listen. I need you to leave. Now."

Rebellion flared on his face. "But–"

"Don't argue. Please don't argue." She tightened her grip on his forearm. "Go back to the others. Run. Don't look back, and don't stop. Tell Rand what happened."

"What about you?" Fear skewed the young man's face. His distress traversed the empathic connection, assailing her already precarious emotional balance.

"I'm staying." She shoved Jasper and reinforced the command, infusing power into her voice so it reverberated. "Go."

He staggered several paces and skidded to a halt. The expression of utter hurt and confusion on his face broke her heart, but she didn't have the luxury of time. If she survived, she would explain and apologize later.

Victoria turned her back to Jasper and walked away, hopefully making it easier for him to leave. She hoped he could overcome his young male need to prove himself just this one time.

Half a block down, Jake waited at the corner, his finger pressed to the walk button in a telling gesture. She quickened her pace to a jog, determined to meet him midway. She refused to show fear or give him a reason to chase her down. As much as she dreaded facing him, as furious and sick as she was over the death of her parents and so many members of her pack, she owed him. The man was entitled to an explanation about how his son had died.

Daniel's blood was on her hands. The guilt consumed her like a cancer, eating her alive.

When she arrived at the corner, the sign indicated no walking, so she chose to wait beside the trunk of a mature ash tree. The wide branches stretched overhead were barren of leaves. Head held high, shoulders squared, she faced Jake with fierce pride and raw determination.

Time ticked past in millennial seconds. At what had to be the world's longest light, they faced one another across the two-lane divide. Vehicles rolled through the intersection, but she barely noticed them. Jake's stone-cold gaze mirrored the smooth, slate-gray surface of his aura.

Shrapnel exploded from the tree trunk beside her face. A sharp wooden shard gouged her cheek. She flinched from the lancing pain beside her eye. The distinctive crack of a gunshot followed the impact.

Her heart slammed against her breast. Wide-eyed, she jerked her face toward the trunk. Hot blood gushed down her cheek before her accelerated healing kicked in and forced the splinter from her flesh. Her flared nostrils caught the toxic fumes of hot silver. Snarling, she ducked just in time to avoid the second shot. The bullet struck the inflatable Santa.

A great whooshing sound accompanied a blast of air from St. Nick's great round belly, and he deflated rapidly. The same shot struck the store's window. Shattered glass rained down upon terrified pedestrians. Voices raised in shouts of confusion and fear. People scattered in every direction, running blindly into the street. Horns blasted, and several vehicles collided.

"Victoria!" Jasper's frightened call carried over the shrieks of the crowd.

"Jasper, get down!" Victoria swung toward the sound of the teenager's voice, desperately searching for him.

"Sawyer! Stop!" Jake's shout cut through the din. The rest of his words were lost to the background racket.

She caught a glimpse of Jasper running toward her, towering at his full height above the hunched crowd. Terrified for him, Victoria sprinted toward the teenager. Once she got close enough, she tackled him and wrapped both arms about his middle. Her momentum knocked him off-balance and toppled him over backward.

Jasper landed flat on his back, gasping as he got the wind knocked out of him. She landed on top of his chest, and he cushioned her fall.

No more shots rang out.

She scrambled to her feet. Gambling precious seconds, she appraised their surroundings. People stampeded in all directions, many seeking shelter within stores. She'd lost track of Jake in the mayhem.

Twisting her head, she searched for the shooter. After a second, she saw Sawyer Barrett, Daniel's brother, bearing down on them at a dead run. The hunter looked to be in the grip of blind fury. Violence etched the lines of his body, and he carried a drawn .45 Magnum.

"Shit." Her heart slammed against her chest. She surged upright, intending to grab Jasper and run, but the hunter was already on top of them. Her action brought her gaze level with the muzzle of Sawyer's gun.

She tilted her head back and stared into Sawyer's face. Overwhelming certainty filled her that her last sight would be his hard blue eyes, burning with animosity. Hatred distorted his handsome features into an ugly mask. "You die now, bitch," he grated. "For my brother—"

A large, fast blur entered Victoria's peripheral vision. Then Jake tackled his son, knocking the younger man clean off his feet. Sawyer's arm jerked skyward, the firearm swung wide, and the .45 went off. The shot boomed.

Around them, humans screamed and stampeded.

Victoria grabbed Jasper's arm and hauled him to his feet. She spared the wrestling hunters the barest glance. She had no idea why Jake Barrett had stopped his son from killing her, and she didn't plan to hang around to find out. Getting Jasper to safety was her utmost priority.

"What's happening?" Jasper asked, staring at the hunters with wide-eyed fascination.

"Keep your head down," she ordered. Dragging Jasper behind her, she set off at a full run due east, dodging people and obstructions. She followed the side street until they reached a narrow alley behind the Western apparel store.

Far fewer people occupied the sidewalk. If they continued to run in a straight line, any hunter with a rifle would have a clean shot at their backs. Yanking Jasper to the right, she shoved him into the alley ahead of her. Her hand slapped his shoulder. "Run!"

"Victoria!" a man's familiar voice shouted.

She cast a frantic glance over her shoulder at the man standing a few hundred feet behind her. She recognized Skinner, a hunter who worked with Jake. She knew the African American man as a passing acquaintance. Before his death, her father had often worked with the hunters who lived in the Phoenix metropolitan area. Acting in concert, wolves and hunters had tracked and slain vampires.

Skinner stood with his arms held tense at his sides, his hand hovering above a holstered firearm strapped to his thigh. He was a large man on the high-side of fifty who looked like someone who broke people in half with his bare hands. Intricate tattoos covered his shaved scalp, neck, and arms.

He had a clean shot at her. She wondered why he hadn't taken it.

"Victoria!" Jasper hissed her name. The teenager remained safely within the cover of the alley but hadn't fled as she'd ordered.

She caught movement from the corner of her eye and realized Jasper was easing closer. She bit back a curse. The teenager was once again placing himself directly in harm's way. If she delayed too long, he'd pop out into the open again. She didn't dare spare the boy an ounce of attention, not while opposed by such a renowned hunter.

Tension vibrated in the air between them. Victoria held his gaze, well aware his eyes would betray his decision to act before he moved. Her breathing slowed. Primal energy coursed through her body, and muscles rippled beneath her skin. She gauged the distance, calculating her speed versus his reflexes. She wasn't sure she could cross the short distance before his gun cleared the holster. A silver bullet would kill her. In a fistfight, no human, not even a skilled hunter, stood a chance against a werewolf's strength.

She'd never killed a real person. Only animals and monsters that sometimes looked like people. She wasn't sure she could start now even if her reluctance cost her life.

"Running won't do you any good," Skinner said in a gravelly voice. "It'll go easier on you and what's left of your pack if you surrender."

Her humanity fell away, and plush white fur pushed through the skin on the backs of her arms, but she retained her human form. A growl trembled in her throat, balanced on razor-sharp incisors. "Take care with how you threaten me or mine, Skinner. I don't want to hurt you, but I will to protect my pack. I'm not easily eliminated. Even if you kill me, I'll come back. I'm Freya's priestess and Odin's Valkyrie."

"The irony is killing me," he said.

She didn't understand his statement and lacked the time to puzzle it through. "I'm taking my charge and leaving."

Skinner's eyes narrowed. A muscle in his jaw jerked. "Nothing is gonna stop Jake from finding out the truth."

"Tell Barrett we can talk." She edged toward the alleyway, holding up a staying hand toward Jasper. She fervently prayed the boy would stay put and not get his dumbass shot. "I'll meet with him just as soon as he gets that crazed asshole under control."

"That crazed asshole is his son."

She clicked her tongue. "I know who Sawyer is."

Skinner chuckled. "Yeah, I'll let him know."

Victoria took his response as a dismissal. Time to go. Before Skinner changed his mind or Jake got through dealing with Sawyer. Determined to escort Jasper to safety, she ducked into the alleyway.

Both hands splayed, she herded the teen ahead of her. "Hurry."

He danced in a circle. "Victoria, that was Skinner, wasn't it? I've heard the stories. Is it true what they say about him?"

She cut him off. "Yeah, that was Skinner. And yes, the stories are true. We're lucky to be alive. Now move before he changes his mind."

"He got his nickname cause he skins–"

"Enough." In an ill-tempered outburst, she delivered a psychic thump with far more force than she'd intended.

Eyes wide, Jasper shut his mouth. His shoulders slumped.

"C'mon." She gentled her tone. "Let's get back to the rest of the pack. We need to warn them hunters are in the area. Then we need to figure out how we're gonna save that little boy. Okay?"

Jasper perked up. "Okay."

CHAPTER 3

Wary of being tailed by the hunters, Victoria traveled south for several blocks and then doubled back. Heading north, she located a drainage canal and left paved surfaces behind. Walking single file, they followed a southeast route across rough terrain and woodsy growth. Even on two feet, their movements were swift and silent, well adapted to the natural environment.

Jasper remained uncharacteristically somber. After a half hour, the silence apparently became more than he could handle. The boy cleared his throat.

Suppressing a smile, she mustered a stern tone. "Yes?"

"Victory?" He pitched her nickname high, turning it into a question.

"What is it, Jasper?" Ducking to avoid the bare

branches of a bush, she cast a curious glance over her shoulder. "We're almost there."

He produced a sound in his throat, a cross between a cough and a huff. "I know *that.*"

She glanced heavenward. As much as she adored Jasper's bold, brash nature, there were moments when he drove her up the wall. *Of course he does. Far be it for me to tell a teenage boy anything.*

Freya laughed. *Victoria, be nice.*

I'm always nice.

Except when you're not.

"I smell coyotes," Jasper continued. "Are there shifters here?"

"There's a band in the area." Victoria scented the smaller canines also.

"Won't they be pissed that we're violating their territory?"

"Maybe. Probably. Who knows what coyotes think?"

Veering away from the creek, she trudged up the embankment. Generally, coyotes weren't a threat to their much larger cousins, but an entire band might just take on a lone she-wolf and a juvenile male if their den was threatened. She didn't want to risk straying too close to their home.

Once they reached the top of the hill, they hopped a chain link fence and landed back on paved city streets. Aging apartment buildings, decaying commercial complexes, and houses with weed-choked yards composed the area.

Jasper rotated in a slow circle, surveying their surroundings. From the distant, confused look on his face, he had no clue where they were.

She took the lead. "This way."

Once they joined up with the other members of their pack, the threat the coyotes presented lessened greatly. Unless the band was huge, they were no match for even her small werewolf pack. She hoped they were smart enough to continue hiding. She and her people had been in town for a day, and they didn't want any trouble. They planned to move on immediately.

Departure grew even more urgent since hunters had found them.

Freya's brightness touched her mind. *The little boy needs your help, Victoria.*

I haven't forgotten Michael, My Lady. Can you tell me where he is?

Perhaps.

Images flickered through Victoria's mind. A cold, cavernous place that might have been a basement. Or a dungeon? Cages suspended upon thick chains hung from the ceiling. Sour dankness flooded her nostrils. The steady *drip drip drip* of water feeding stagnant puddles echoed through the emptiness. Most disturbing, the mewled cries of frightened children calling for help.

Terrible dread coalesced in Victoria's gut. *There's more than one child?*

I believe so.

Who is the child thief?

In response, Victoria received another nightmarishly surreal vision. A sinister figure that stood upright on ungulate legs and had many attributes of a beast. Flared horns. Black fur. Cloven hooves.

She huffed. *I'm hunting a giant goat?*

The stream of pictures stopped. *I don't know what it's called. I'm sorry.*

Michael's still alive?

For now. You must hurry, Victoria.

"I'm hurrying."

Glancing over his shoulder, Jasper shot her a curious look. "Are you talking to Freya?"

Victoria bobbed her head once. Unfazed, he shushed. Her people knew her well. Her occasional, inexplicable outbursts were par for the course.

They entered a poor residential neighborhood adjacent to an industrial district. A rubber recycling facility loomed over the surrounding area like the silhouette of a silent giant. Stacks of black tires rose higher than the ten-foot chain link fence that surrounded the complex. The dense column of black smoke indicated the presence of an active incinerator. Thick smog of tarry residue, pesticides, and other gasified toxins hung over the area.

To their sensitive noses, the air smelled and tasted like death.

"It stinks." Gagging, Jasper covered his nose and mouth and jaywalked across the busy street.

Victoria followed without protest. Gathering her resolve, she broached the matter utmost on her mind. *Goddess, why didn't you warn me Jake Barrett would be here today?*

She waited, but no answer was forthcoming.

Goddess? At last, she sighed and shelved the matter. Freya wasn't obligated to provide explanations. Victoria's independent streak made blind obedience difficult. She'd been a priestess since she'd turned fourteen, but still she struggled with the obligation to maintain an unquestioning faith in her goddess.

As they cut across a gas station parking lot, Victoria's phone rang. She dug the device from her pocket. The pack had taken to using cheap prepaid mobiles so they couldn't be traced. "Hello?"

"We're gettin' antsy." Rand Scott's lazy Southern drawl filled her ear. "Where the hell are y'all?"

"Turn around, worry wart."

A few hundred feet away, Rand Scott, Victoria's second-in-command, spun on his prosthesis leg. Over seven feet in height and at a weight in excess of three hundred pounds, the enormous Beta wolf boasted a build like a grizzly. He bristled from head to toe with fiery ginger hair, including a thistle of facial growth that obscured his lips. His thick eyebrows formed a solid unibrow. Years before, his leg had been severed in a motorcycle accident.

"Aww, hell!" Rand bellowed.

Laughing, she waved and ended the call.

Still holding his phone, Rand's hand dropped. His ruddy face skewed into a fierce scowl, but his light eyes gleamed with mirth. Allegedly, he was the runt of the litter. To hear him tell it, all four of his brothers were bigger and meaner. One was even the Alpha of a prominent pack. Yet for all his attempts to project a fearsome demeanor, the man had the disposition of a Labrador retriever.

"Sorry we're late," she said, walking toward him.

"About damn time," Rand grumbled. The molasses quality of his voice removed all the bite from his words.

Jasper shot past Victoria, sprinting ahead. "We ran into hunters! We barely made it out alive. You won't believe..."

Victoria muffled a snarl of irritation and continued at a sedate pace. She should have warned the teenager to let her break the news, but thoughts of the hunters and the missing boy had distracted her.

Rand's head cocked inquisitively. "True story? You ran into hunters? Or is the boy just screwin' with us?"

She shielded her eyes and peered up at Rand. "True

story. Let's have everyone gather round so I can tell the tale once instead of several times. We're pressed for time. I'm gonna need everyone's help."

Jasper's shout attracted the pack's attention. They gathered in the center of the convenience store parking lot that served as their temporary base of operations. With funds being so tight, the seven of them were living out of their two vehicles. Victoria performed a head-count and confirmed everyone was present and accounted for.

Aside from herself and Rand, five others composed their group. Paul and Sylvie Thornton were a mated couple in their sixties. Sixteen-year-old Morena was a year and three months older than Jasper, but the girl never allowed him to forget it. Finally, pregnant gray wolf Sophia, the only non-shifter in their ranks.

They assembled between the parked cars. Rand assumed a position to Victoria's right, standing with his arms crossed over his chest. She wasn't sure whether he did so deliberately, but she appreciated the display of solidarity. Aside from Rand, she didn't face any potential challengers for her position as Alpha from within the pack.

Sylvie and Paul also stood. The Native American woman had a tall, strong stature and kept her gray hair pulled back into a neat ponytail. She acted as their Skald, the keeper of tradition, and was a devout follower of

Freya. Her husband was a battle-scarred warrior who had lost a hand and a leg in conflicts past.

Morena sat beside Jasper on the lowered tailgate of Paul's truck. The teenagers dangled their long legs, feet swinging frantically back and forth. Sophia also occupied the bed of the pickup. The gray wolf lay with her head resting on her front paws. She had lost her mate in the same massacre that had slaughtered most of the Storm pack. Werewolves often took regular humans or wolves as their mates, and the pups she carried in her belly were the product of such a union. They had the potential to grow into normal wolves or shifters. Each one carried the shape changer genes which could be passed on to future generations. They were the future of the pack.

Victoria told the whole story. She began with the appearance of the restless ghost-mother and went on to share the plight of the missing boy. Then she recounted their confrontation with the hunters and the escape that followed. The others listened intently. Even the rambunctious teenagers held their questions until she finished.

When she got to the exciting part with the shooting, Jasper smirked and gloated while Morena gasped and clutched his arm. The pair sat close, thighs touching. *Too close.* Victoria frowned. They'd have to be chaperoned closely to ensure their relationship progressed no further. At their age, infatuation was easily mistaken for true love. Casual sex could result in the pair forming an unbreakable mate bond. In her estimate, they were too immature to enter into such an immense commitment

Rand waited until she finished her explanation, then asked, "Any idea how Jake found us so quick?"

Victoria noted how easily Rand used their enemy's first name. Not Barrett. Not the Hunter King. *Jake.* He harbored no fear of the vaunted hunter, and she longed to get him alone to question his attitude.

Of course, Rand had worked with the hunters hundreds of times. In Phoenix, vampire incursions were frequent and vicious. For over thirty years, wolves and hunters had been staunch allies. The two disparate groups often worked together to defend their mutual and overlapping territories.

"We discarded our cell phones. Changed the plates on the cars. Stopped using credit," Paul said, frowning. "What did we miss?"

Victoria cleared her throat. "I'm not sure we missed anything. When he first saw me, he looked surprised. I don't think he knew we were here."

"*Es obvio, ¿no?* Freya sold us out." Morena sat with her back rigid, her legs no longer swinging. Her dark eyes glittered, and her chin jutted. Whether her words were true or not, the girl's accusatory tone was completely unacceptable.

Jasper recoiled from her as if struck.

Victoria opened her mouth to deliver a sharp reprimand, but Sylvie beat her to it. "Morena, bite your tongue! How dare you speak such blasphemy."

Their communion surged with the disapproval of the adult wolves. Rand and Paul contributed their full strength to the consensus, but they left the decision to the Alpha. With minimal effort, Victoria nurtured the discordant note until it reached a crescendo. A nudge sent it crashing over Morena.

Before the will of her elders, the teenager's defiance crumpled. Her gaze dropped to the ground, and her shoulders slumped. Her voice quavered as she apologized. "I'm sorry. I'm scared. I just want to go home, but there's no home to go to anymore."

Victoria traded a sorrowful glance with Sylvie. Morena had lost her parents and her older brother in the Phoenix massacre.

They'd all lost someone.

Sylvie approached Morena and placed her arm over the girl's shoulder. "Shhh, it's okay, sweetie. I know you're upset but you can't lash out like that, especially against our goddess."

Red with embarrassment, Jasper scooted off the tailgate and edged toward Paul. All three of the pack's males suddenly seemed to find the sky interesting. Victoria wasn't much more comfortable. Morena's outburst mirrored her private doubts all too closely.

"We should talk about splitting up again," Victoria said. "It would be in everyone's best interests."

Heads jerked her way, expressions ranging from shock to outrage.

Rand stomped his good foot. "No. No fucking way. I promised your father I'd look out for you."

"Listen, please." Victoria held up staying hands, and at the same time, exerted her will over the pack bond to soothe volatile tempers and ease fears. "We all know Jake Barrett is only after me. If we approach one of the other packs, I'm sure they'd accept refugees. Rand, your brother is Alpha of–"

Rand growled deep in his chest. "Don't mention that bastard to me! *Ever.*"

Fuming, Victoria shut her mouth. Stupid, stubborn male egos would be the end of them all. "Fine. There are other packs. The children would be safe. Sophia could have her puppies in a proper den..."

Cradling the back of Morena's head, Sylvie glared at her. "Our answer now is the same as it was last week, Victoria Svana Storm. We won't be leaving you, and you won't be leaving us. We're family."

United in their resolve, the pack put their foot down, a force to be reckoned with. They were solidly loyal to her. Bashful pleasure bubbled up inside of her. Despite everything, a smile tugged at the corners of Victoria's mouth. She might be Alpha, but her father had always said a wise leader bowed to the will of his people.

She schooled her voice to a let's-get-going tone and clapped her hands together. "Well, since that's settled, let's figure out how we're going to locate Michael. It'll be faster if we split up. I want to check out the library to see if there's anything in the local newspaper about his disappearance. Showing up and asking at the police station would attract too much suspicion. Everyone else should stay together."

A warm blast of approval radiated from the others. Thankfully, her people were a practical lot. They returned to business as usual.

Sylvie patted Morena on the back and then tilted away. "We should all stay together. Our strength is in our numbers." She clenched her arms across her chest.

As quick as a whip, Morena leapt onto the lowered tailgate and Jasper returned to his spot beside her.

Paul itched at the gray scruff on his jaw with his good hand. "Victoria's making the best compromise she can between protecting the pack and trying to save this boy."

"I don't object to saving the boy, but we have our own children to look after." Sylvie sent a pointed glance toward Morena and Jasper. "We have another month or so before Sophia births her cubs. She and her pups will need a den to hole up in for the first month. It will be another two months before they are able to travel."

"I haven't forgotten," Victoria said softly. "I will find a safe place for the pups. I promise."

"I vote with Victory." Absently, the burly redhead reached down and scratched the top of Sophia's head.

Sophia opened her mouth wide and whined with pleasure. Then the gray wolf rolled onto her back for belly rubs.

Victoria scowled. "This isn't a democracy."

"It's a Victorocracy!" Morena piped up with a bright, false smile. Dark blues streaked her aura, blending into stormy gray clouds.

Jasper dug his elbow into her side. "That's stupid!"

Morena punched him in the arm. "Is not! *Eres estúpido!*"

"Is so!" Jasper took a playful swing at the girl.

Laughing, the pair tumbled across the truck bed, wrestling for dominance. Morena and Jasper shared the lowest status within the pack: Omega, the least dominant wolves. Their youth kept them from establishing a respectable rank in the pack. A perpetual state of rivalry existed between them.

Watching the teens, Victoria rolled her eyes and smothered a smile. She did her best to appear disapproving, but her amusement spread and touched the others. Soon, every adult grinned while the oblivious teens squabbled.

"Look, I understand the situation is dire." Victoria met

the gazes of each individual in turn, but she addressed them as a whole. "The hunters have us far outnumbered and outgunned. If the pack is to survive, we have to avoid any more confrontations, even though it goes against our nature. We are descended from the great wolf-god Fenrir. We are Vikings."

"Aye, we are." Rand flashed a fierce smile that showed off all his teeth. He pumped his fist in a punching gesture, reinforcing the message. His bolstered morale blended seamlessly with hers.

"We are also Blackfoot," Sylvie said, making a gesture inclusive of both she and her husband.

Paul rumbled deep in his throat. "First and foremost, we're wolves. Sylvie, my love, we are an honorable people. At the behest of our goddess, this spirit has sought our help to save her son. If we abandon a helpless child, we are no better than cowards."

Sylvie stared into her mate's eyes. Her face flushed, then a reluctant smile curved her lips. "You are right, my love. We must save the child."

Suspicion edged Victoria's thoughts. Sylvie was seldom swayed from her views. She wondered if the Skald had played devil's advocate on purpose. Whatever the case, the weight on her shoulders lifted, and she breathed easier. Of course, she could have issued a command, but handing down orders did not suit her. She preferred to have her pack's cooperation and consent.

"Can I come along?" Jasper squirmed, giving the impression he might burst at any second.

Morena elbowed him in the side. "No fair. I want to go!"

Jasper slapped her arm away. "I called it first!"

"I'm older," Morena shot back.

Victoria frowned. "No, it's too dangerous. Both of you are staying here."

"That's not fair!" Denied the opportunity to prove himself, Jasper succumbed to anger and disappointment. His volatile emotions roiled through the empathic connection.

Rand rumbled with deep laughter. "I'll go with you."

"That works." Victoria agreed with an eager gleam in her blue eyes. If she had to have a wingman, she preferred Rand. Even with a prosthetic leg, the brawny redhead fought better than both of the teen werewolves put together.

"Good, we're agreed." Victoria addressed the entire pack. "Rand and I will start with the library and then proceed from there. Everyone else needs to stick together and maintain a low profile. Stay close to the vehicles. If things go south, be ready to leave at a moment's notice. If we get separated, we'll meet up in Santa Fe."

CHAPTER 4

In the downtown area, Albuquerque's Main Library offered convenient hours and access to public computers. Hunched over a keyboard, Victoria searched the Internet for information on the missing children.

Rand peered over her shoulder. The huge redhead occupied a wheeled office chair that squeaked and groaned beneath his weight.

"Will you stop breathing down the back of my neck?" She moused over the most promising result and clicked on the hyperlink. A painfully slow data load began.

"I'm not."

"You are."

He chuckled. "What's got you madder than a wet hen?"

"I'm not." Victoria shot a glare at him.

Rand's mouth stretched into a crocodile smile.

The news site finally loaded, so she returned her attention to the screen. She read the article and summarized for her companion. "This was published in the Friday morning edition. June Fraiser was murdered sometime Thursday night. It says her six-year-old son, Michael, is believed to have been abducted by the same person who killed his mother."

"Does it say anything we don't already know?"

Only the tightness choking Rand's characteristically lazy drawl hinted at inner turmoil. She recognized his restrained anger. His reaction closely mirrored her own emotions.

Squinting, she continued reading with furious intent. The tension between her and Rand built to an intense pitch rather like the droning buzz of a mosquito. He remained silent and waited for her to finish without making further interruptions.

Huffing, she sat back in her chair. Dread filled her gut, her worst suspicions confirmed. "More than one child has been abducted."

A growl rumbled in the Beta wolf's throat. "How many?"

"Four over the course of two weeks. Michael was the most recent." She committed the abducted children's names to memory and printed the article.

"Have they found any..." Rand's voice crunched like crushed glass.

"Not yet. We may be able to save them." Victoria offered a silent prayer to Freya. She opened a new tab in the web browser and performed another search of an online directory. The results yielded a home address for the murdered woman. She sent a second job to the printer.

"I'll grab those." Rand rose from his chair.

"Thanks." Victoria hastily closed out the web client and logged out.

They joined up again in the main lobby and left the library just after 3:00 p.m. A glance passed between them, and silent communication flowed across the pack bond. His question. Her affirmation.

Furry brows arched, Rand nodded.

Concordance resonated between them like a single perfect note. By mutual consent, they climbed into the pickup and headed to the crime scene.

THE SECOND-STORY WALKWAY overlooked the complex's courtyard which was made of red pavers. Thorny bushes and weeds crowded lava rock-filled planters. The buildings showed signs of considerable disrepair–peeling paint and drooping siding. Potholes pockmarked the parking lot, and graffiti covered the surrounding walls. The tenement was located less than a mile from where she had encountered the murdered woman's spirit.

"Two-twenty-two. This is it." Rand stopped, eyeing the trio of tarnished brass twos that hung off-center above the mail slot.

"Yeah, this is it." She knocked on the red door.

"Forty-eight hours is a long time for a little boy to be alone with a killer." Following a short delay, he tried knocking also.

"Yes, it is." Victoria shuddered.

Rand had just voiced her darkest fears. Her blood ran cold at the thought of a terrified child in the hands of a monster. Freya's vision haunted her, especially the frightened cries of youngsters.

"Looks like no one's home." He reached out and twisted the door knob which didn't open. "It's locked. Should we force the door?"

Victoria chewed her lower lip while she considered. She had been raised in the suburbs as part of a middle-class family. Her worst criminal offense to date was speeding. She had no idea how to pick a lock and had certainly never trespassed on a murder scene before. Of course, she and Rand were both strong enough to bust the door down, but she was uncomfortable doing so.

She bent and lifted the welcome mat. "Maybe there's a hidden key."

Rand snorted. "We should be so lucky."

"I've got nothing." She lowered the mat into position. She balanced on the tips of her toes and tried to reach the top of the doorframe, but it proved just out of her reach.

He snickered. "Don't strain yourself, little buddy."

"Watch it, Rand." She bared her teeth in a warning snarl. She had never lived down the fact that she had reached her full height of less than five feet at the age of twelve.

"Damn, Victory, no need to be so fucking sensitive about your height. No one minds you being an itty-bitty–"

Victoria jammed her elbow into his side. "Shut up."

"Ouch. Fuck!" Holding a protective arm over his ribcage, Rand flashed a shit-eating grin. He ran his free hand along the top of the doorframe.

"One more smart remark about my height, and I'll ram that peg leg up your ass."

"Hey, now. No need for violence." His face lit with the delight of discovery. "Ah-ha!"

Her brow shot up. "Really?"

Rand held up a brass key. "Oh yes. Really."

"Dumb luck." She smothered a grin. She enjoyed Rand's company. Although he had forty-six years to her twenty-four, she felt closer to him than Morena and Jasper. Life, and particularly recent experiences, had aged her beyond her years.

He inserted the key into the lock before he hesitated. "Not sure it's right to enter a police crime scene. I hope we don't mess nothin' up."

"Don't worry. It's not an active forensic investigation scene or there would be an officer posted. After the police are done, they leave it to the property owners to clean up."

Rand shot her a perplexed glance. "How do you know that?"

Her voice flatlined. "I dated a cop for a year."

He winced. "Oh, yeah. Sorry."

"It's okay." She shrugged. If Rand knew she was lying, he kept his mouth shut for a change. She was grateful for his rare discretion.

Daniel had worked as a Sheriff of Maricopa County, Arizona. He'd been gone just over two weeks, and his death still didn't feel real to her. Every morning she woke and opened her eyes, expecting to be in her own bed, to roll over and see his dark head resting on the pillow beside her. Her heart ached as though it had been cut from her breast. The deaths of her parents and so many others compounded her pain until she had emotionally shut down. The pack needed her to remain strong, so she chose numbness over grief and focused on survival.

Rand shoved the door open and entered the apartment first. He cocked his head, nostrils flaring and nose twitching. "Yeah, someone sure as hell died in here."

Following on his heels, she gagged when the revolting scent of decay assailed her sensitive nose. A wave of nausea swept over her. "Hit the lights."

"Yeah, gimme a sec." His hand slapped the wall a couple times before he found the light switch beside the door, and a dim table lamp came on. The illumination sent dozens of cockroaches skittering along the floor and walls.

Victoria's expression twisted into a grimace. She followed Rand inside and closed the door behind them. The small apartment had a galley-style kitchen, one bedroom off the living area, and one bathroom. The dried out husk of a Christmas tree stood sandwiched between an old television and a bloodstained couch. There was no mantle, so two felt stockings dangled from the kitchen counter. One still had a dollar-store tag attached.

"June must have died here." She bent to touch a couch cushion. She skimmed the gummy surface and her fingers came away dry. She spotted a curious bloodstain on the carpet and knelt to inspect it. The basic shape suggested a cloven hoof. A trail of similar marks led toward the bedroom.

"Whatcha lookin' at?"

"Are these footprints?" She pointed to the stains.

Rand's brow pinched. "Sure as hell looks like it."

Victoria's lips compressed, and she lowered her face

to floor level. She inhaled deeply, and a pungent scent filled her nostrils. "I smell goat. I think."

Rand pressed his face to the ground and closed his eyes, huffing deep breaths while he learned the smell. He looked up and frowned. "I'd say bighorn sheep."

She snickered. "You like sheep, don't you, Rand?"

"Hey!" Rand's head reared back, and he took a lazy-pawed swipe at her which she easily dodged. Laughter rolled from the big redhead.

She stood and followed the trail toward the bedroom. "What sort of goat-scented monster murders mothers and steals children?"

"Beats the hell out of me," Rand said, scratching his beard. "Satyr, maybe?"

"This isn't Greece." She leaned into the apartment's single bathroom. She switched on the light and gave the room a cursory inspection: one sink, a toilet, and a bath-tub-shower combo.

"How should I know?" Rand rolled his massive shoulders. "I've fought vampires and the occasional demon. Saw a kachina spirit once outside of Flagstaff, but it wasn't harming anyone, so we let it be."

"Smart man." As she returned to the hallway, she caught him giving her a peculiar look. The corner of his mouth curled upward, so his eye pulled into a squint. She stopped. "What is it?"

"Running into Jake Barrett has got you in a snit," he said with uncanny astuteness.

She winced and bristled, feeling unaccountably defensive. "The man and his hunters murdered my parents and most of our pack. Of course I'm unsettled. I shouldn't have to remind you."

Following Daniel's death, Victoria had taken his corpse to the Barrett residence. Sawyer greeted her with guarded curiosity until he saw the condition of his brother's body. Without waiting for an explanation, he grabbed a shotgun and attacked her. She barely escaped with her life. The incident had set the hunters and wolves, allies of thirty years, on the brink of war.

The next day, Victoria's parents and most of the adults of her pack had met with Jake Barrett at a private airstrip outside Phoenix. Her father had ignored her objections and forbidden her to attend. He ordered her to escort the pack's young, infirm, and vulnerable members to safety. Rand accompanied Victoria as her second-in-command.

None of her pack mates who attended that fateful meeting ever returned. All were dead, including her mother and father. No one except maybe Jake Barrett knew exactly what happened. The news stations carried a story about the explosion of a fuel truck at the airstrip. Allegedly, the resulting fire killed dozens, including human hunters. Following her Alpha's orders, Victoria took the people under her protection and ran.

"Uh-huh." The look Rand gave her said he didn't buy her excuses even for a second.

No matter what, her guilt and grief weren't topics for casual conversation. Jaw jutting, Victoria shook her head. "Don't want to talk about it."

"All right." Rand turned toward the final doorway to the one room they hadn't inspected yet. "This must be the bedroom."

Victoria entered ahead of him and turned on the lights. The small room contained a double bed and a five-drawer dresser. A toddler bed and a toy chest stood against one of the walls. Lego blocks and Matchbox cars littered the floor. The space hardly seemed big enough for one person to occupy, let alone two.

"I thought you said the boy is six," Rand said, scowling at the toddler bed.

"That's what the spirit and the newspaper said. I guess it's what she could afford." Victoria pitied the dead woman and missing child more than ever. The boy had lost everything. She hoped they could save him.

"Where the hell is the boy's father in all this?"

"The article said she was a single mother. No mention of a father."

Rand walked past the beds and examined the room's only window which had been broken inward. The vinyl mini blinds lay in a mangled heap on the floor. Glass fragments littered the carpet. "This is where it entered. I only smell the one creature."

She bent and picked up a small red fire truck off the spotted carpeting. She inspected the toy and then tucked it into the front pocket of her jeans. The threadbare comforter on the bed contained a lumpy polyester fill. She committed the boy's scent to memory and then wadded the blanket into a ball.

"Catch," she said, tossing it toward Rand.

"So there's no one left to miss the poor kid?" Rand caught the blanket out of the air and held the blue fabric to his nose. After a few seconds, he returned the blanket to the bed.

"No, probably not." She shook her head in sorrow. If they failed to save the boy, she would feel responsible for his death, the same way she already felt for so many others.

Rand stilled, and his gaze settled on her. "Cut yourself some slack, kid," he said in a gruff tone. "Everything isn't your fault."

Her stomach dropped. She stared at him.

"Isn't it, though? Daniel is dead because of me." She had known dating a hunter was reckless and off-limits, but that hadn't stopped her. "Dad knew Jake Barrett would blame me for his son's death. It's why he kept me from attending the meeting with the hunters."

"Ah, so you get to claim credit for the massacre at the airfield 'n starting the fighting too, I suppose?" Rand's brow arched. "Something of a royal screw up, aren't you?"

Tears stung her eyes, and a hot flush of temper set her teeth on edge. "Mocking it doesn't make it any less true."

"Course not," he drawled. "But it might help you see the only person blaming you for what happened is you. The pack doesn't hold you culpable for any of it."

Her anger dissipated and left her flushed with embarrassment. His reassurance served to undermine her self-confidence. She was a failure as Alpha. She lacked the necessary experience and wisdom to serve as a good pack leader. The role had been thrust upon her years before she should have been ready.

"Rand." Uncertainty threaded her voice, vibrating with the strength of her curiosity. She had a question she wanted—no, *needed*—to ask but did not know how to phrase it.

"Just spit it out."

She sighed. *Fine.*

"Why haven't you challenged me for Alpha yet? We both know, in a fight, you'd win. You're older, more experienced, better suited to leadership."

Rand laid a hand on her shoulder. Victoria tilted her head to gaze into his face. She fully expected her question to finally provoke the ritual challenge.

He scowled. "I was loyal to your father and mother.

My Alphas. So I'm loyal to you, Victoria Storm. If your father had wanted me to be leader, he'd have put me in charge."

"Alpha isn't a hereditary title, Rand. It has to be earned."

"Let me guess. You don't feel you've earned it?"

She shook her head.

His nostrils flared as he exhaled. "There has been a Storm leading this pack for five hundred years. You're a good leader, just a little bit inexperienced. You need to stop being so hard on yourself."

Victoria opened her mouth, although she had no idea what she intended to say. Before she formulated words, her cell phone rang. She sighed, extracted the mobile from her pocket, and checked the number.

Sylvie.

"Victoria," Sylvie said in a voice filled with panic. "It's Jasper. He's gone."

An awful sense of foreboding filled her, but she strove to remain cool. "Jasper was upset when we told him he couldn't come with us. He's probably just sneaking around after me and Rand."

Beside her, Rand snorted. "That boy needs his backside tanned."

Victoria waved a silencing hand at him. "Don't worry, okay? We're through here. We'll come back and track him down."

"Okay." Sylvie's tone calmed. "Please hurry."

"We will." Victoria put the phone away and looked to the redhead.

Rand rolled his eyes. "Well, fuck. I guess we'd better get after that little shit."

"Rand, don't be too hard on him, okay? He's just a kid."

"It's time for him to grow up and start being a man." He accompanied her outside and closed the door of the apartment behind them. "Do you have a plan for finding Michael?"

"Not yet." A sense of urgency coalesced in her gut. The need to act grew imperative, but she had no idea what to do. "C'mon, let's go."

Together, they returned to the parking lot where they'd left the truck. Rand approached the driver's side of the pickup and unlocked the door.

"Smells like a storm," he said.

As if to echo his words, thunder rumbled miles in the distance. The clouds formed a thick gray blanket. Orange hues tinted the horizon, and a brisk breeze blew easterly.

Victoria tilted her head back, scenting the moist air. "It blew up suddenly. I didn't know it was supposed to rain."

"It wasn't. Not according to the weather report I read this morning anyway."

She traded an ominous glance with Rand, and their shared concern remained unspoken. Picking up a scent trail that was already a couple days old was difficult in an urban area. Rain would destroy any chance they might have had of doing it the old fashioned way.

They drove for a couple minutes. A light drizzle started, just enough to turn the dust on the windshield to mud. Rand turned on the wipers. The rain wasn't heavy, but it was enough to obliterate any trace of a scent trail Jasper might've left. His disappearance ate at her. She hated her inability to act, and each passing minute stretched like an hour. The teenager hadn't been gone for long, so she doubted he'd gotten far. Most likely, he'd return to the pack once he'd blown off steam.

The consolation offered cold comfort.

CHAPTER 5

Fretting over Jasper's safety, Victoria chewed her lower lip and stared out the window at the passing scenery. In many ways, Albuquerque was like Phoenix. Certainly, the landscaping and architecture of the high desert city reminded her of home. Small discrepancies such as unfamiliar local businesses and vegetation really stood out. Those differences served to sharpen the knowledge that she could never go home again. Even if they managed to make peace with the hunters, she couldn't return to the place full of so many painful memories.

From that first date with Daniel, she'd known becoming involved with a hunter was wrong, but she hadn't been able to resist him. When he asked her out, she'd gone in defiance of good sense while questioning his motives and her own the whole time. She didn't hide that she was dating a hunter from her parents or pack. However, they'd kept their relationship a secret from Jake Barrett and the rest of his family.

The first time Daniel broached the issue had been a rainy Sunday morning in April. He lay sprawled across her queen-sized mattress with the headboard and a stack of pillows propped behind his torso. His dark eyes followed her every move as she dressed in medical scrubs. She had an upcoming shift in the emergency room of Good Samaritan Hospital where she worked as a nurse.

"Call in sick. Play hooky with me." Daniel wore a wicked smile and a sheet tangled around his hips. His tanned skin contrasted sharply with the white cotton. He lacked tan lines, even in the middle of winter, a fact she teased him mercilessly about.

"I can't. People are counting on me." She frowned to hide her amusement. In the few months they'd been together, she'd learned that indulging his antics only made his behavior worsen. She certainly didn't want him to know just how much the offer to climb beneath the covers with him tempted her.

"What time are you off?"

She perched on the edge of the bed and pulled on her shoes. "I'm working three consecutive twelve-hour shifts in the ER. Then, I have plans with friends Thursday and pack business on Friday. I'm visiting my parents Saturday."

While she tied the laces, he rolled onto his side. His hand snaked across the mattress and caressed the curve of her backside through her blue scrubs. "I don't want to have to wait a week to see you again."

Victoria didn't like it either, but she put on a cool smile and evaded his grasp. Glancing back, she said, "You'll live. Besides, it keeps the sex interesting."

Daniel's brow furrowed, and he sat upright. Anger honed his features and sharpened his scent. "We've got more than sex going for us."

Startled, she stood and turned to face him. "Sure, we have fun together. I couldn't ask for a better hunting partner."

They worked together well as a team. To avoid other hunters, their expeditions often took them to remote, isolated areas outside the city. They preferred to stalk and destroy vampires. Undead were unusually common in the Phoenix area. They'd also taken on the odd ghost, and what might have been a chupacabra... Or a member of her pack playing pranks. They'd never figured *that* one out.

Daniel surged off the mattress. His wide stance and the position of his shoulders reminded her of a wrestler. His aura shimmered with vibrant red-toned swirls. "You just don't want to admit that we're good together."

"Whoa, hold up there, lover." Her hands rose to his abdomen, and she smoothed her palms across his sides. "We're good together. That's not the issue at all. And you know it."

Beneath her touch, he stilled. His heartbeat slowed, and his respiration steadied. An elusive empathetic resonance buzzed in the air between them, strong enough so she felt his restrained anger. The connection wasn't as intimate as the pack bond, but it held tantalizing promise.

Resolve hardened in his eyes. He placed a finger under her chin and raised her face so only inches separated them. Their breath mingled, and the moment became as intimate as a kiss.

Her breath hitched. Mentally, she crossed her fingers and prayed he wouldn't do this now. She wasn't ready to have the big commitment talk yet. They hadn't been dating long enough for her to even be sure how she felt about him. For every reason they should be together, a dozen real world considerations existed to keep them apart.

"Daniel–"

He held her gaze. "I'm going to tell my father about us."

Upon hearing him say it aloud, her alarm spiked. His intentions were as she suspected and as she feared. She liked things as they were between them. She didn't want everything to change. Her grip on his sides tightened. "No."

"Victoria, we need to discuss this." His jaw twitched near the corner of his mouth. The set of his shoulders, as well as every nuance of his body's posture, bespoke staunch determination. The man was a force to be reckoned with when he set his mind to something.

Exhaling, she let go of him and took a step backward. "I don't have time for this right now. I need to leave or I'm going to be late for work."

"When then?" His jaw tipped in a stubborn jut. "When do you have time?"

"Call me tonight." She shot him a long, unhappy look. He hated being put off, but she expected him to be reasonable. He couldn't upend their entire dynamic and expect her to adjust at a moment's notice. "Please don't go ruining what we've got. I want to enjoy it while it lasts."

Face set in an implacable mask, Daniel stared at her for a long time before he opened his mouth to answer—

"We're almost there."

Rand's voice cut through her reverie, yanking Victoria back to reality.

Choking on painful emotions, she twisted to face the redhead. "Let's hope Jasper is back."

"Yeah." His reply carried a distinct note of doubt.

Striving to escape her dark musings, she slanted a look toward her companion. Humming along in off-key concert with a tune on the radio, Rand appeared unperturbed. Curiosity ate at her. She had questions about his attitude toward Jake Barrett and dying. She didn't know how to phrase them without insulting him.

"What's eating at you, kid?" Rand asked in a gruff voice. He never took his eyes off the road.

An automatic denial formed, but she hesitated to offer an outright lie. Lacking a tactful approach, she blurted out, "You didn't seem worried earlier."

"I'm not the worrying sort." He shot her a speculative sideways glance without bothering to disguise his curiosity. "What about?"

"Jake Barrett."

"Oh." He snorted. "Yeah, well. I worry for the rest of the pack, but not about Jake killin' me."

Her eyebrows knit. "You think he won't?"

"Nah, that's not it." Rand's chuckle reverberated in his chest like a rusty engine. "I don't worry about dying. All the dumb ass shit I've pulled. Never figured to live as long as I have."

Her alarm spiked. "You're not even fifty."

"Fifty is old." He flashed a teasing grin. "I want to die fighting. Hopefully while I still can."

Victoria scowled. "You think Barrett would be a worthy adversary and an honorable death?"

"Not think. *Know.* I've accompanied the man on countless hunts."

The pickup rolled to a halt at a red light. Tense silence endured while they waited for the signal to change. The whole time, Victoria bit her tongue against the desire to call Rand an idiot.

His attitude didn't surprise her. Her people followed the old ways. Enemies had driven Loki's wolf shifter children from their Old World homeland centuries before. They fled to North America. However, they worshipped the ancient gods and clung to their Viking heritage. The only good and honorable death came as a courageous end in glorious combat. The victims of murder, sickness, and accidents were all doomed to the gloomy underworld. Certain exceptions were made for women who were deemed worthy and a place was created for them in Freya's hall.

She not only accepted the doctrine, but embraced it. In addition to being Freya's priestess, she was a Valkyrie who transported the souls of the chosen to Odin's Valhalla. So she wondered if her reaction was entirely selfish. She depended on Rand's strength and his experience. Losing him would make the already difficult job of pack leader even harder.

The light turned green, and the truck lurched into motion again. The light drizzle continued to fall. Water beads danced on the side windows and then stretched into long streaks across the glass.

"Relax, kid. I'm not going anywhere," Rand said at last. "I don't intend to commit *Hari Kari*."

"Don't even think about it." She adopted a fierce glare and menaced him with her fist, playing it for laughs. She didn't want him to figure out how much the prospect of losing him scared her.

"I won't." Chuckling, Rand turned the pickup into the parking lot of the convenience store and pulled into a space. He shut off the engine.

A cool smattering of rain pelted Victoria when she climbed out of the cab. Inclement weather was unpleasant, but not a big deal. As wolves, they were capable of enduring much worse. The SUV was parked a few spaces over. Sophia appeared in the rolled up window of the vehicle. She rested her paws on the sills, pressed her nose to the glass, and peered out.

Side by side, Rand and Victoria walked around the rear of the truck to greet Sylvie. The older woman hurried toward them. Worry lines etched her face, and muddy swirls marred her tranquil aura.

"Thank the goddess you're back," Sylvie said. "Jasper's not answering his cell phone. I'm afraid something awful has happened."

"Don't panic. I haven't felt anything through the pack bond." Victoria adopted a soothing tone and projected confidence. Her gaze strayed past Sylvie to Morena. The teenager lurked next to the SUV's quarter panel, staring intently at a spot on the ground.

"How long's he been gone?" Rand scratched at his beard. His knowing gaze also settled on Morena.

Sylvie worried her lower lip. "He must've taken off right after the two of you left for the library. I was hoping he followed you."

"Without a car? Not a chance." Rand shook his head.

"Where's Paul?" Victoria asked, needing to know the locations of every member of her small pack. The bond wasn't the equivalent of mystical GPS. Unless Jasper experienced severe emotional distress or injury, she couldn't use it to track him.

"He's looking around the neighborhood for Jasper," Sylvie answered. "In case he just wandered off to blow off some steam."

Victoria stepped past Sylvie and approached Morena. The teenager slumped against the SUV's quarter panel. Her gaze fixated on the ground. At her Alpha's approach, the girl visibly shrank in upon herself, arms crossed in a self-hug. She stank of guilt and fear.

Victoria stopped in front of her. "Morie, did Jasper tell you where he was going? If you know, you need to tell us. It's too dangerous for him to be out there alone. No one's going to be angry with you."

The teen produced an indecipherable whimper. She trembled from head to toe.

Victoria settled her hands on the teen's shoulders and steadied her. "Morena?"

Morie's head rolled to the side. Tears streaked her cheek. "I told him not to go. I told him it was stupid. But he said he needed to prove he's an adult or no one would ever take him seriously."

A cold rush of fear swept through Victoria. Swallowing panic, she caught the girl's eyes. "Where is he?"

With a snotty inhalation, Morena scrubbed at her eyes. "*Lo siento.* He made me promise not to tell."

"Tell me. *Now*." Biting back a growl, Victoria asserted her will through the pack bond and assumed command of Morena's wolf. The girl cowered before her.

The Omega sank to a crouch, conveying her submission to her Alpha. "Jasper had it all figured out. He said Jake Barrett was surprised when he saw you. If he was surprised, then it must mean he wasn't expecting to see you, which means he's in town for some other reason."

Sylvie and Rand both shifted restlessly.

Victoria sucked in a sharp breath. An awful suspicion filled her, so scary she prayed she was wrong. Striving to keep her voice steady, she asked, "What other reason?"

Morena sniffled and scrubbed at her face with her sleeve. "He said Freya sent you to that exact spot to talk to the ghost mom of the missing kid. Since the hunters were there too, they must be after whatever grabbed the boy."

"Hell." Victoria glanced up at Rand and Sylvie. Both of her pack mates looked gob smacked. From the *oh-shit* expression on their faces, they arrived at the same conclusion.

Sylvie said, "That's smart."

"Yeah, it is," Rand rumbled. "Makes sense."

"Why didn't we think of it?" Victoria released her hold on Morena's shoulders, relinquished her tight control over her wolf. She straightened to her full height.

The burly redhead scowled. "We're id–"

Victoria waved her hand. "Don't say it."

Rand flashed a toothy smile. "Sure thing, boss."

"Smart ass." Her wolf roiled beneath her skin, threatening to burst through at any moment. With an effort, Victoria unclenched her jaws.

Sylvie stepped closer to Morena and placed an arm around her shoulders. "You did the right thing by telling us, sweetie."

"I'm sorry. I should have said something sooner, but I didn't want to be the reason he gets in trouble," Morena whispered, clinging to Sylvie.

"He's not in trouble, sweetie."

Alarm threatened the foundations of her composure. Victoria backed up until she collided with Rand. Biting her tongue, she addressed her anger to Freya. *When I get hold of that stupid boy, I'm going to make him regret having been born.*

Victoria, he is a child. You must be patient.

Rand's huge hand dropped onto her shoulder. His strong fingers dug into her skin hard enough to hurt, communicating the fear he refused to voice. "If he's shadowing hunters, we'd better find him before he gets his damn head blown off."

Victoria latched onto Rand's arm and dragged him to the edge of the parking lot. She didn't want Morena to overhear them. "I agree with you about finding Jasper. First, we need to find a new place to park the vehicles. We were only supposed to be here for an hour or so while I carried out Freya's mission. Sooner or later the police are going to notice we're loitering. Once there's radio chatter, the hunters will know exactly where we are."

Rand's eyes narrowed, and he spoke in a hushed voice. "You're right. We don't want to draw any unwanted attention to ourselves. Jake Barrett has all kinds of government contacts."

"We need to find Paul," she said. *Damn it all to hell.* Victoria hated the prospect of moving before they'd located Jasper. If the teen returned to the convenience store, he'd have no idea where they'd gone. As Alpha, she had to consider the greater good. She couldn't endanger everyone for the sake of one stubborn, reckless boy.

"He's here." Rand's head turned, his gaze fixated upon

a point over her shoulder. "Looks like one thing's going our way today."

Victoria swiveled and breathed a sigh of relief upon sighting Paul's approach. The older man's limp was more prominent than usual. He looked tired but none the worse for wear. She noticed he clutched a piece of crumpled yellow paper in his hand.

Rand got out in front of Victoria and beat her to Paul's side. Grinning, the redhead extended his arm. "Let me help you, old man."

"Get yer damn hands off me. What the hell is wrong with you?" Waving his fist, Paul menaced the Beta wolf. "What's going on?"

Chuckling, Rand fell back. In the space of a heartbeat, his grin vanished, replaced by a fierce scowl. "We think Jasper's trailing the hunters in hopes of finding out more about the missing boy."

Paul's brow shot up over wide eyes. "That's dumber than some of the shit you've pulled, Rand."

"Yeah, well. What can I say?" Rand spread his hands wide in a gesture of assumed innocence. "I set a high standard. The kid's really gotta aspire to follow in my footsteps."

"All right, both of you, that's enough." Victoria smothered a reluctant smile.

"Aye, boss." Despite his cavalier sense of humor, Rand

had a solid head on his shoulders. His jocularity ceased, and he fell into sync with her.

"There's something you need to know." Paul waved the piece of paper he carried so it produced a stiff crackling.

CHAPTER 6

"There's more than one missing child." Arm extended, Paul proffered the flyer.

Victoria stared at the weathered paper and then reluctantly accepted it. She quickly scanned it. She recognized the girl's name from the newspaper article. Margaret Anne Wazzle, age 10. The missing child notice included the black and white photocopy of an adolescent girl and cited a few grim facts. The bodies of the parents were found in their bedroom. The murderer was suspected of having abducted the girl from her home.

As she read, an awful sinking sensation swept through her. She had no idea how to go about finding the abducted children or the child thief. The crisis associated with Jasper's disappearance had temporarily diverted her attention. Now the emergencies were closing in from all sides.

Composing her thoughts, she offered up a prayer. *Goddess, if I'm to find these children, I need more to go on.*

A hesitation ensued before Freya responded. *I would tell you exactly where to find them if I knew. However, there is a shroud preventing me from knowing their location.*

"Before you showed me the glimpse of a vision, but it was too brief," Victoria said, desperation edging her voice. "Can you show me again? Please? Maybe there's something I missed."

At her outburst, Rand and Paul exchanged a knowing glance. Neither man commented. Her pack mates were accustomed to her seemingly one-sided conversations with the goddess.

Freya hesitated. *I held back. Some of it is horrific. I have shielded you on purpose.*

Freya's obvious reluctance aroused Victoria's suspicions. Her already pessimistic expectations plummeted further, leaving her cold inside. Bracing for the worst, she asked, *Goddess, is Margaret still alive?*

Sorrow colored Freya's golden voice. *I'm sorry, Victoria. The girl is already lost.*

Victoria ground her teeth so hard her jaws hurt. *Show me.*

It is sordid.

Goddess, please. I have to know what sort of monster I'm up against.

It is what you want?

"It's what I want." Unsure what to expect, Victoria braced by stiffening her legs. Seconds later, a vision slammed her. Her five senses overloaded under the deluge of information. Overwhelmed, she dropped to her knees and pitched forward, reflexively extending her arms. Her palms smacked the rough pavement, and she gulped air. A cold drizzle pelted her head and back, and her soaked clothing hung heavily on her slender frame. She lost awareness of her own body.

The pillow beneath Margaret's cheek was wet from the tears she'd shed. Her heart ached for the shattered furry body they'd found in the gutter in front of the house. Her beloved cat, Carmen, hit by a driver who hadn't bothered to stop. She suffered the agony of grief. But the awful, suffocating guilt was even worse.

Her mother's voice played over and over in her mind. "It's your fault the damn cat's dead, Margaret. If I told you once, I told you a million times not to let that animal run past you. It serves you right she's dead! Maybe you'll finally learn."

Her mother was right, she was an awful person. She hated herself for being so irresponsible. If she'd been paying attention, then Carmen wouldn't have run past her into the street. The car wouldn't have hit Carmen and she'd still be alive. She *hated* herself.

It was all her fault.

Everything.

Torn apart by the force of her sobs, she cried herself into exhaustion and eventually fell asleep.

She woke to her mother's shriek and her father's deep shout. Their cries shattered the hush of the slumbering house. A terrible growl resounded, and then the screams ended abruptly. Adrenaline coursed through her body. Her throbbing heart pushed against her throat with every beat, threatening to choke her. Terrified, she pulled the thick down comforter over her head and shrank beneath the covers. Shivering, she curled into a fetal ball and closed her eyes, wishing herself invisible.

Heavy footsteps clomped in the hallway outside her bedroom. She shook so her teeth clattered, and she clenched her jaws to stop the betraying sound. A floorboard creaked in the hallway outside her bedroom door, and the intruder stopped moving.

She bit her lower lip so hard that salty blood flooded her mouth. Tears stinging her eyes, she held her breath and clutched the blanket in both hands. *Please, please, please... Go away, go away, go away...*

With the crack of shattering wood, the door to her room burst inward. Huffing, the monster thudded toward her bed. She screamed as the blankets were ripped away, her only protection stolen, leaving her vulnerable and exposed. Lying on her back, she stared up wide-eyed at the enormous beast standing over her. Darkness obfuscated its appearance except for a pair of malevolent glowing red eyes.

The monster seized her legs and dragged her from her bed. She kicked and screamed to no avail. A heavy, leathery hand clubbed her upside the head. Pain exploded throughout her skull, the world spun, and she sagged in its bruising grip.

The beast grabbed her, shoved the mouth of a large burlap sack over her head, and stuffed her into the bag. Her weight settled at an uncomfortable angle so she lay on her bent neck. She hurt from head to toe. The thick, scratchy material itched, and the hot interior stank of urine, vomit, and terror.

She struggled weakly for a while, but physical exertion made it harder to breathe. After a time, she gave up and grew still. She lay in a limp heap listening to the ominous stomping of the monster's steps as it carried her down the stairs and from the house. Tears streamed from her eyes. Snot clogged her nose and throat. The humiliating wetness of her nightgown told her she'd peed herself.

In the distance, cars honked and engines revved. Another awful smell grew more potent, competing with the others. The burnt, tarry odor was familiar. She walked past the tire recycling facility every day on her way to school, and she despised the place. The black smoke always made her cough worse and left her short of breath. Her mother blamed her daughter's asthma on the factory.

Her abductor upended the sack by grasping the bottom. He shook it until she slithered out. Shrieking, she fell several feet to a concrete floor. The side of her skull slammed against a sharp surface and her mind swam with wavy lines of consciousness. Her whole body hurt. She lacked the strength to move.

The monster loomed above her, a dark and shadowy form.

"You must be punished for your sins." The lyrical voice dissolved into maniacal laughter. He carried her toward a steel drum filled to the brim with opaque fluid. He stood so much taller than her that her feet dangled far off the floor. She couldn't gain any traction.

"Mommy! Mommy! Please! Help me!" Shrieking, she flailed her limbs. His strength far eclipsed hers. She couldn't escape his grasp. The surface of the vat loomed before her face. The bitter scent of ink assailed her airways, and she choked on the stench. As her scream ended, he forced her face into the liquid. Darkness eclipsed her vision. Horrible pain burned in her eyes.

Reflexively, she inhaled. Fluid filled her mouth and throat, crushing her lungs. Terrified beyond reason, she sobbed and thrashed with all the strength in her frail body. Taunting, gleeful laughter filled her mind. The monster drank her sorrow and fed on her fear.

Her life force shrank.

Darkness.

Margaret simply stopped. Fighting. Breathing. Living. Being.

"Breathe, kid!" Rand's shout assailed Victoria's eardrums. He shook her like a rag doll in the grip of a great dog. His anger crashed through the pack bond like a rampaging bull, decimating everything in his path.

His open hand struck her cheek. Shocked, she opened her eyes. Rand's face loomed over her, contorted with panic, and his voice boomed over her. Still, the terrifying press of suffocation threatened to crush her. She gasped, fighting to draw a breath. Her heart thundered, and her lungs ached. Rand drew back his arm, and then his open palm smacked her cheek again. Her head whipped to the side, and Victoria gulped air into her starved lungs.

Expression thunderstruck, Rand lowered his hand. "What the hell happened?"

Victoria struggled to formulate words. The Beta wolf's steady presence helped fortify her composure. She grabbed hold of his arms to steady herself. At her core, horrified revulsion crystalized into fierce resolve. As a she-wolf, the brutal assault against a youngster was the worst possible sin imaginable. *Goddess, I'm going to find this son of a bitch and disembowel him with my teeth.*

Good. Freya's approval burned through Victoria. The goddess shared her primal loathing of a beast that preyed on helpless children.

"You okay, kid?" Rand prompted her.

She licked her lips and said, "I'm fine."

Rand rocked on his heels. "Sure don't look fine to me."

Victoria patted his forearms, offering reassurance. "Seriously, I'm fine. " Belatedly, she realized the others were huddled around her. Glancing at each, she studied the worried faces of her pack mates. Not just Paul and Rand, but Morena and Sophia crowded close to her also. They weren't a large pack, but their members were tough. Their strength bolstered hers.

She was so incredibly grateful for each and every one of them.

"Did the goddess reveal the location of the missing boy?" Sylvie asked with thinly veiled impatience.

"I have it," Victoria said. "I know what area to search for the stolen children."

"Good." Paul stood beside Sylvie, staunchly supporting his mate. "Where do we look?"

"Not we. Me," Victoria said. "We're going to have to divide up to cover as much ground as possible. I need Rand to go after Jasper. Sylvie, Paul, I want you to move the vehicles to a safer place."

Dissent rippled through the pack bond. Mouths opened in protest. Eyes gleamed with rebellion. Through their communion, she sensed that the others disliked her plan down to the last wolf. Only Morena was too full of shame to object.

Victoria braced, fully expecting a challenge to her leadership. Her self-doubt didn't help her confidence any. Aside from being the daughter of the deceased Alphas, she possessed no qualifications as a leader. She had less life experience than Rand, Sylvie, or Paul. So who was she to tell them what to do?

Exhaling, Rand released her and took a step back. "I'll take the truck 'n go after the brat. If I find him, you can rest easy that I'll haul his sorry ass home."

Before he finished speaking, Sylvie and Paul stifled their disagreement and lent their support. Solidarity crystalized within the pack; unity of purpose to the attainment of shared goals.

Victoria breathed a sigh of relief. She didn't have the strength to fight her own people *and* deal with the myriad external threats. "Thank you, Rand."

He grunted and tipped his head in acknowledgement. The ghost of a smirk hovered on his lips, gone before fully manifested.

"How far should we move the vehicles? And to where?" Paul asked. "Are you sure you don't want us to wait?"

"It's not safe." Victoria shook her head, recalling how close of a call she'd had earlier in downtown Albuquerque. Jake wasn't in shoot-first-ask-later mode, but he wasn't the only hunter. There were others, including Daniel's younger brothers. The maddened expression of rage on Sawyer's face haunted her memory.

Following a terse debate, Sylvie and Paul agreed to take the SUV and get on the highway, heading toward Santa Fe. Once beyond city limits, they'd find a safe place to stop and hole up with Morena and Sophia until the pack managed to reunite. Rand would follow in the pickup as soon as he located Jasper.

"How're you supposed to join us?" Morena asked, finally breaking her silence. The teenager stared at Victoria with wide, worried eyes.

"Don't worry. I'll catch up." Victoria mustered a smile for the girl. "If I have to, I'll summon Bifröst." Technically, she wasn't supposed to use the rainbow bridge for matters unrelated to her duties as a Valkyrie. Given the circumstances, she hoped Freya would make an exception.

You know I will. Why don't you just ask?

Victoria smothered a smile. *It's easier to apologize than to ask permission.*

The goddess sighed. *Someday your propensity for questioning authority will get you into trouble, Victoria.*

"Have you thought about what you're going to do

when you find this creature?" Rand asked, eyeing her with plain trepidation. "No offense, kid, but you're not exactly built for monster slaying."

"Gee, thanks." She scrunched her nose. "Both of you. Stop giving me a hard time."

Rand's brow arched in fleeting confusion before realization dawned on his face. Then he grumbled. "You should listen to your goddess."

Laughter was Freya's only reply.

"Let's get moving," Rand grumbled. "Time's a wastin'."

RAND PULLED the pickup truck alongside the shoulder of the road and stopped in front of the tire recycling facility. He twisted around to face Victoria and glared from beneath bushy red eyebrows knit into a fearsome scowl. "Be careful. If you need help, call me."

"Will do, Auntie Rand." Snickering, Victoria opened the passenger side door and slid from the truck. The light drizzle continued to fall, but her clothing was already soaked through. More rain hardly mattered. She closed the truck's door and watched while he drove away.

Once the taillights faded from view, she followed the chain link fence, walking the perimeter of the enclosed yard. Her hopes of picking up a scent trail proved futile.

Aside from the rain, the stench of burned rubber pervaded the area.

She completed her circuit, having found no breaks in the fence or easy ways around the barrier. A thick chain and heavy padlock secured the front gate. Looking up, she considered the ten-foot climb which included a roll of barbed wire at the top.

With her wolf's strength, Victoria could jump it without much difficulty. However, she questioned whether a massive creature like the child thief would be capable of leaping so high. She suspected the entire structure would topple beneath his massive weight. And how would he make the climb while hauling along a sack containing a ten-year-old child?

There were other places she could look–commercial shopping complexes, industrial areas, and tenements. Even the gully wash she and Jasper had cut through would offer isolated places for the beast to make its lair. A search on foot would take forever. She had to find some way to narrow the area down.

As if in answer to her dilemma, a coyote's cry cut through the night. The speaker was a young female who had complaints about a padlock on a grocery store dumpster.

Victoria turned toward the sound which came from the direction of the creek. She judged the coyote to be less than a half mile distant. Perfect. Just the help she was looking for. She hoped they were friendly and not fiercely territorial. A band of coyote shifters stood a reasonable chance of taking down a lone she-wolf.

She had to gamble.

Tilting back her head, Victoria raised her voice in a nimble, polite howl of greeting. She supplied her name, rank, and pack, and then allowed the pure vocalization to fade. She cocked her head and waited.

Following a brief hesitation, a male coyote replied, cautiously welcoming. *I'm Alpha of the Albuquerque City Slickers.* His introduction ended on a high note of inquiry. *What do you want, wolf?*

The tip of her tongue darted across her dry lips as she swiftly weighed her words. Before she'd introduced herself, she hadn't stopped to consider that the band could be in cahoots with the child thief. A stupid mistake and one she couldn't retract. Following a brief internal debate, she decided to follow her initial instincts.

Summoning her power, Victoria infused her song with her own personal magic. She shared the heart-breaking visions of the kidnapped children and the few details she had of the monster. Her howl embodied loathing and loss, imperative and immediacy.

The coyote Alpha's howl cut her off mid-refrain. *Are you going to kill the bastard?*

Based on the proximity, he was moving closer to her.

Annoyed at the interruption, she swallowed her pride

over the insult to her honor. Practicality demanded it. Besides, no one expected coyotes to respect social niceties. With equal brusqueness, Victoria viciously roared, *Yes.*

He waited until the curl on her snarl faded before he released a short series of yips. *Talk to the mutt in the alley behind the grocery store.*

Victoria scowled. "Asshole," she muttered. "I've got no more idea where the grocery store is than I do–"

Across the street, a man stepped into the open, emerging from some overgrown bushes. His tattered clothing included a long coat that hung to mid-calf. The garment concealed his build. He was bigger than her, though that was true of almost everyone.

"I'm Silver," he said. "Only my friends are allowed to call me asshole."

"Hate your name," Victoria said in lieu of a greeting.

Long silvery hair hung in a tangled mess about the coyote shifter's face and shoulders, obscuring his features. His smoky baritone smirked. "Yeah, well, you're the trespasser in my territory."

Even at a hundred feet, Victoria's nose confirmed he wasn't as unwashed as one would've assumed at a glance. Grunge seemed to be his personal style rather than the artifact of poverty. She bared her teeth and beckoned him with a crooked finger. "You want to challenge me or tell me where to find the damn monster?"

"Go about a mile that way." With a graceful sweep of his long arm, he pointed with one finger. "There's a stray dog that lives in the alley behind the grocery store. He can take you to the beast."

"Why don't you show me?" Appraising him, Victoria stepped into the street. To his credit, Silver held his ground. "Better yet, how about helping me kill it?"

"Not my problem, especially not with hunters in the area," he said with a curl of aggression in his voice. "Besides, a wolf doesn't need mere coyotes, does she? You have your pack..."

"It's murdering children."

He stiffened, and his scent soured with anger. "Not my problem."

"Coward." Victoria hissed, exhaling between clenched teeth. Her hair and clothing were drenched, she hadn't eaten in two days, and the lives of children were endangered. She didn't have time for this bullshit.

"I like living."

Disgusted, she turned away from him. In a deliberately scornful tone, she tossed over her shoulder, "Thanks for the help."

"Hey! We aren't through." Silver's volume spiked. His steps splashed through puddles on the pavement as he followed her.

"We're through." She kept walking, hiking in the direction he'd indicated. With any luck, he hadn't lied. The bright spot in the whole awful situation was the moment when the rain finally ceased. Although, it wasn't as if her soaked clothing could get any wetter.

Swift footsteps trailed her. "I can't risk the lives of my people for a bunch of human kids."

"Whatever." She picked up her pace, dropping into a swift run.

Up ahead, she spied a strip mall that had a small food retailer as the anchor store. The market wasn't far from where she'd met June Fraiser's spirit. Ghosts tended to either haunt the scenes of their deaths or an area with powerful emotional significance.

"Rumor has it, Jake Barrett's in town," Silver called out from behind her.

"I know." She dropped to a walk. "We think he's here after the child thief."

"Funny." He scoffed, ratcheting the noise to a full throated laugh. "We figured he was hunting wolves."

Pointedly ignoring him, Victoria looked around. A couple lonely vehicles occupied the otherwise deserted parking lot. Tall lamps cast long streaks of light that stretched across the glistening wet pavement. All the businesses were already closed, and their employees had gone home.

She spun toward Silver. "Is this the right place?"

He rocked back. "Yeah, this is it. You'll find the mutt in the alley around back. He lives behind the dumpsters."

"Thanks for the info." She arched her brow and stared. The unruly tresses concealing his face prevented her from capturing his gaze. When Silver skulked away, a hollow pang of disappointment filled her belly. At the same time, her reaction puzzled her. She wasn't naive. Coyotes had reputations as resilient survivors, not foolhardy heroes.

Following the paved sidewalk, she rounded the corner and entered the alley behind the stores. Posted signs designated the area for deliveries. An eight-foot brick wall lined with steel dumpsters ran the length of the business complex. Despite the recent rainfall, the area smelled like motor oil and rotting garbage.

When she entered the backstreet, a rumbling growl emerged from between two trash bins. Victoria swung toward the sound. Her posture flowed to a predatory stance, prepared and close to the ground. By scent, she identified the source of the sound as another canine.

A big dog emerged from the shadows, menacing her with a constant rumble and bared teeth. His ruff bristled, and he walked stiff-legged. He had the black and tan markings of a Rottweiler, but the shape of his head and body suggested he was a Shepherd mix.

"Hey, boy," Victoria said, adopting a soothing tone. She dropped to a crouch to appear less threatening. The animal was big but posed no real threat to her.

With his ears flattened against his skull, the dog

postured and barked furiously at her. He advanced even closer, growling deep in his throat.

"It's okay. I'm not going to hurt you." She extended her hand and stared into his eyes, exerting her influence as Alpha to calm his fear.

Gradually, the dog's anxiety decreased and then ceased altogether. His ears rose to high points, and his stubby tail quivered. He sniffed suspiciously at her proffered fingers and blew moist, hot breath across her skin. When he identified her scent as that of a far more dangerous predator, a tremor traveled the length of his body.

He adopted a submissive posture, so his head sank lower than hers. His tail stump wagged furiously. Whimpering, he crept closer to lick her fingers. Rudimentary empathy flickered between them. Wolves weren't so different from dogs that she couldn't feel his loneliness and hunger.

"There's a good boy. Are you all alone?" Victoria checked his neck and found no collar. She ran her palms over the dog's sides, tracing the indentation of his ribs beneath his mangy coat.

The Rottweiler whined, asking for food.

Victoria's stomach rumbled in sympathy. "You're hungry, aren't you? Poor baby. I'm so sorry I don't have anything for you. It's been a while since I've eaten too. If I survive this, I promise I'll find you something to eat that's not trash."

Cradling the dog's head between her hands, Victoria captured his gaze. She bolstered the delicate empathic connection between them. The magic required caution and precision. She couldn't afford to risk accidentally making a stray mutt a member of her werewolf pack. It could happen if she wasn't careful. The teenagers wouldn't mind, but Sylvie would have fits.

"I'm looking for someone, a monster that hurts children." She whispered, projecting a strong visualization of the child thief across the psychic link. What she lacked in detail, she made up for with other sensory specifics, including the clomping of the beast's footsteps.

Shaking, the dog moaned and pressed closer to her. He returned impressions rather than words. Fear and refusal. His thoughts contained images of a bad place that stank of the sorrow and the terror of children. *Stay away.*

"No, I'm going to kill it. Once I'm through with this thing, it won't be able to hurt anyone ever again." She projected cool confidence. Mastery. "Take me to it."

The dog's resistance collapsed. Head held low, he skulked along the alleyway, pausing to glance over his shoulder. The message was clear: *follow.*

She stood and trailed the dog. He led her along a circuitous journey through back alleys and side streets to a strip mall a few blocks south of the grocery store. When he halted in front of a business, Victoria also stopped.

"Is this it, boy?" she asked.

The dog answered with a short bark, warning her against danger. She received the strong impression of affirmation, but also fear and concern.

"Thank you." She patted his head, projecting approval. She sensed how badly the dog wanted to leave. She said, "It's okay. You can go now."

The big dog stood rooted in place, tremors wracking his body. Victoria sensed his internal conflict–fear warring with loyalty. His instincts for self-preservation were at odds with his desire to follow and protect her.

A cynical smirk twisted her lips. "I'll take one of you over five coyotes any day." Reaching out, she asserted her will on the dog and commanded him. "Go."

Whimpering, he turned and retreated toward the street.

Examining the store front, Victoria made a mental note of the address. She tilted her head back to read the name of the restaurant: Karp Sum Chinese. The decal of crossed chopsticks over a fortune cookie was etched into the front window. An Out of Business sign hung in the front door.

She tested the front door and found it locked. For a second, she contemplated ripping it off its hinges. A child's life was at stake, so the element of surprise gave her an advantage. She chose stealth over brute force.

Circling around to the rear took her into another alleyway lined with trash bins. She located the back door and was surprised to find it standing ajar. A thin sliver of light shone through the crack.

Before she entered the building, Victoria took out her cell phone, set the device to silent, and returned it to her pocket. Turning sideways, she slid through the narrow opening. Within, she picked up the same musky, ungulate odor she'd smelled at Michael's apartment.

Her stomach growled.

Sighing, Victoria rolled her eyes. She entered a back room filled with crates and boxes stacked atop pallets. Shelves full of assorted containers bore a coating of thick dust. Exposed duct work and pipes covered the ceiling and walls.

Silently, she padded forward, using the stacked pallets as cover. Her nocturnal vision adjusted to the dimness. Her eyes cast a golden glow, illuminating her path. Her hands shifted to claws tipped in wicked nails, and her teeth elongated to sharp canines.

The soft sob of a child drew her onward. She hid behind a large steel drum. The pungent goat-scent permeated the entire area along with the stench of urine and feces. The fetid aroma overwhelmed her sensitive nose. Still, she caught the unmistakable underlying scent.

Human children.

She peered over the edge of the open drum. The container was filled to the rim with black fluid. Curious, she dipped a finger into the liquid and lifted it to her nose for a quick sniff. When she identified it as ink, her face contorted into a grimace of distaste.

Victoria extended her thoughts to Freya. *Goddess, what is this sick bastard?*

It is an abomination, Priestess.

Four wrought iron cages hung on chains suspended from the ceiling. Three contained small children: two boys and a girl. At a glance, they were between the ages of three and six. Shock hit her in the gut, leaving her winded and paralyzed for precious seconds. A wave of nausea assailed her. The thought that she'd almost refused to come to their rescue appalled her.

The heavy clomp of hooves on concrete alerted her to the monster's location on the far side of the room. A bipedal creature stepped into view. It stood over ten feet in height. A pair of curved horns flared from its skull. Red-rimmed eyes were deep set within its elongated face. It had a broad nose, a small mouth that formed a nasty grin, a bearded chin, and elven ears.

Male genitalia dangled between hairy legs that belonged on an ungulate. Cloven hooves created a distinctive clomp on the concrete. Thanks to Margaret's nightmare, that sound was indelibly burned into Victoria's imagination. As long as she lived, she'd remember the poor girl's absolute terror as the beast approached her bedroom door.

Wiry black fur covered his entire body. A thick mane grew on his head and shoulders, thinning across his sides and arms, only to thicken again upon his thighs. He had a five-fingered hand tipped in razor-sharp nails. A whip-like tail grew from his tailbone, and the beast stood hunched over due to the curvature of his spine.

Hostility vibrated throughout her, and she primed for violence. She hesitated out of fear for the youngsters. She doubted her ability to take on the immense beast in a one-on-one fight and win. The creature outweighed her by hundreds of pounds. If she died here, the knowledge of the goat man's location died with her. She needed help and regretted her decision to send Rand away.

An unexpected wave of fear and panic knocked Victoria off-balance. Gasping, she fell backward. She immediately identified Jasper as the source of the distress. She swallowed an instinctive snarl, instead producing a strangled gurgle in the back of her throat. Her wolf surged to the surface, threatening to burst through her skin.

A second later, Rand's fury roared across the pack bond. Adrenaline surging, Victoria crouched behind the barrel and struggled to regain control. Through an act of willpower, she managed to impose a degree of composure. Scrambling, she headed for the rear entrance, intending to call her pack mates once she reached safety.

Sides heaving, she stepped into the alleyway. A blinding burst of pain slammed her, and she stumbled. *Rand is hurt.* Her shoulder struck the side of the building and kept her from falling. She dug her phone from her pocket, but her hands shook so hard she fumbled. It took her two tries to clear the screen saver. Before Victoria had a chance to dial, the phone's screen lit up with an incoming call from an unknown number.

She answered automatically. "Hello?"

Only silence and the crackle of white noise emerged from the speaker. She started to speak again, when a man's rough voice asked, "Victoria?"

She froze, and her blood ran cold.

Jake Barrett.

CHAPTER 8

Her grip on the cell phone tightened, knuckles turning white. Twisting, she scanned the area around her but saw no sign of hunters. Surprisingly, she caught a glimpse of the Rottweiler peering at her from the far end of the alley. The dog had defied her command and followed her.

"I know this is your number." Jake's tone conveyed strength and authority.

He sounded so damn much like Victoria's own father that it hurt to hear. She struggled to wrap her dry mouth and tight throat around words. "Is Rand still alive, Barrett?"

"Rand knocked around a couple of my men. Didn't kill anyone. I know him well enough to know he could've." His intonation remained perfectly cool and reasonable. "He took a shotgun blast to the chest. Unfortunately, he took off in a pickup before I got there."

Victoria released a held breath, dissipating awful internal pressure. It went without saying the hunters hadn't been using silver slugs or Rand wouldn't have survived a direct hit. Let alone escaped.

"Why would he attack your men?" Victoria asked even though she instantly supplied her own answer. *Jasper.* Rand must've been defending the teenager.

"That's the crux," Jake said. "I've got your boy."

Fear impaled her heart. Victoria sank to a crouch, kneeling on the wet pavement while her wolf fought to drag her through a full shift. Thunder filled her ears, and she thought the storm had returned until she realized the sound was a growl rumbling deep in her chest.

They spoke simultaneously.

"Barrett, where is Jasper? So help me, if you've hurt him—"

"The boy is unharmed. As long as you do what I say, he'll be fine."

Her grip threatened to crush the phone. Fumbling thanks to her claws, she wedged the phone between her shoulder and jaw. "So, the mighty Hunter King has sunk to taking children hostage?"

Jake's voice thickened with irritation, the first crack thus far in his impenetrable veneer. "I didn't go after the boy. We caught him shadowing us."

"What do you think Daniel would think of you right now?" The snarl never wholly left her throat, so the demand reverberated.

"Don't you dare speak my son's name, *bitch*." His control cracked, betraying smoldering fury.

"I'll tell you, he wouldn't think very highly of you." She ignored his warning. Taunting the man wasn't the smartest thing. Her fear for Jasper drove her to recklessness.

Grinding teeth, a noise like stone on stone, crossed the phone line. He exhaled, and her imagination supplied the image of broad flared nostrils breathing fire. When he spoke, his tone was smooth once again. "My son is dead. Someone has to be held accountable. I expect you to surrender yourself. Once you have, I'll let the boy go."

Fuck. The man terrified her. No matter what Jake Barrett did to her, it couldn't be worse than the suffocating guilt she lived with every day. The weight of her own culpability in Daniel's death crushed her, a feeling verging on self-hatred. Too many people on both sides had already died because of her failure. She would do anything to protect the final surviving members of her pack, including sacrifice herself. Perhaps it was fitting that Jake Barrett should be her judge, jury, and executioner.

"Fine. I'll surrender to you," she said. "I want your

word that Jasper and my pack go free without any further retaliation."

"Agreed." A hesitation ensued.

She thought her ready agreement had surprised him. She stepped into the silence before he could continue. "We have another problem."

Jake's volume shot up a couple telling notches. "We do, do we?"

"The monster you're hunting is here."

His voice hardened with suspicion. "What makes you think I'm after anyone other than you?"

The bones in Victoria's hands crunched as she forced her claws to retract. She gnashed her teeth in irritation. "On the street you were surprised to see me."

"Maybe I was surprised you made it so easy."

"Maybe," she shot back. "Maybe you're not interested in killing the murdering bastard. Oh, he's got three little children in cages. No reason that should concern–"

"It's not smart to keep needling me, Victoria."

Victoria's phone lit up with an incoming call from Sylvie. "I've got another call I have to take."

"Don't you dare–"

With a smirk of satisfaction, she put him on hold and accepted the other call. "Hello?"

"Rand's been shot," Sylvie said without preamble. "He got away, but the hunters have Jasper."

"I know." Victoria composed her voice to offer reassurance. "I've got Jake Barrett on the other line."

Sylvie fell into stunned silence. A full thirty seconds passed before she said, "You put Jake Barrett *on hold*?"

"What's he gonna do? Kill me twice?"

"No. He may take his frustration out on you before he does."

Victoria flinched. Sylvie's stinging reminder punctured her bravado and deflated her ego. Her head dipped in shame. The Skald had the right of it. She'd foolishly allowed wrath and pride to get the better of her. She exhaled. "I'm sorry. You're right. Let's make this quick. Is Rand going to be all right?"

"Yes, he's badly hurt, but he'll recover. It'll be hours before he's recovered enough to be of use to you."

"Where are you now?"

"A few miles north of that tire recycling facility."

"I thought you and Paul were supposed to have left town," Victoria said, her tone heavy with irony. "What happened?"

Sylvie's voice lilted. "We stopped for gas."

Despite the direness of the situation, Victoria laughed. "Take everyone and head to Santa Fe. This time, *please*, do what I ask."

"What about you and Jasper?"

"I'll take care of it."

Sylvie hesitated. "How?"

"Sylvie, please, trust me," Victoria pleaded. She didn't have time to argue or explain. Her newfound leadership style entailed indulging her people's questions. She ran her pack as a democracy with an elected president rather than the autocratic dictatorship of a larger war band.

"Of course, sweetie. Call soon so we don't have to worry."

"Thank you," Victoria said in heartfelt relief and gratitude.

"No, thank you."

They said their goodbyes and concluded the call. Victoria switched back to Jake. The first sound she heard was the rasp of his breath on the line. His impatience and frustration coalesced as a palpable force.

"Let's stop playing games, Barrett," she said. "Are you hunting the child thief or not? I know where it is. It's got three young children in cages. If you're not going to help me kill it, then say so."

Silence ensued. Victoria imagined those thick gray Barrett eyebrows knit into a scowl of consternation. She smirked. The man had devoted his life to hunting and destroying the monsters that preyed on innocents. There was no way he would walk away from this fight.

"Yeah," Jake rumbled. "A friend of mine brought the matter to my attention. It's why I'm here. We've been looking for it for a few days without any solid leads."

"It's enshrouded in some sort of magic," Victoria said.

"That makes it difficult to locate." Her supposition was conjecture, but the facts thus far supported the conclusion.

"How'd you manage to locate it then?"

"Deductive reasoning and a keen nose."

He snorted softly. "How did you get pulled into all this?"

"My goddess sent me."

"Of course she did."

The amusement in his voice irritated the crap out of her. Unaccountably, tears welled in her eyes, and her voice cracked. "The first little girl the beast took, her name was Margaret. It murdered her parents, shoved her into a filthy sack, and drowned her in a drum of ink."

Jake growled. The sound was indistinguishable from a wolf's, and if she hadn't known better, she'd have assumed him to be one of her people.

Her anger burned so hot her wolf was about to burst through her self-control. "It murdered her for what?" she asked. "The poor girl was innocent."

"Have you seen it?" He bit the words short.

Victoria drew a deep breath and described the goat-creature to him, going into great detail. His knowledge of the occult was far superior to hers. Her father had once called Jake Barrett a walking, talking encyclopedia of the arcane and obscure.

He cut her off mid-description. "Sounds like a krampus."

"A what? Never heard of it." She shook her head even though he couldn't see her. Her mind was so deep inside the conversation her awareness of the external world faded.

"It's an Old World devil," Jake said, adopting a brisk manner, devoid of animosity or any hint of the bad blood between them. The man possessed an amazing ability to compartmentalize. "Originally from Germany and Austria, but its kind has spread throughout Europe. It's a child thief. It steals children who have been naughty and then punishes them. It feeds on guilt. I've never heard of one in North America before."

"Do you mean 'devil' literally or is that a figure of speech?" Victoria adjusted her stance, flexing her knees to stop them from cramping.

"It's complicated."

She scowled. His evasion sounded like a total... hedge. They'd attained a degree of concordance though, a certain unity of purpose she was loath to disrupt. Besides, what ultimately mattered wasn't what it was, but rather how to destroy it.

"Does it have any weaknesses?"

"Not like your people do to silver."

She winced at the pointed reminder. "How do I kill it?"

"Tell me where you are," Jake said. "I'll kill it."

His vicious conviction sent chills coursing along her spine. She absolutely believed that he'd do as he said. The man had a reputation as a ruthless killer who possessed powerful magic. He demolished any and all obstacles in his path. He never failed.

She gave him the address.

"Wait until I get there," Jake said in an unmistakably autocratic tone.

Her brow drew together. Under the best of circumstance, Victoria disliked being told what to do. Being ordered about by her enemy didn't sit well. "I'll think about it–"

Loud barking erupted from the far side of the alley. Startled, Victoria looked toward the sound and lowered the phone. The Rottweiler stood at the end of the building. His posture bristled with aggression.

"What's wrong, boy?"

"What's happening?" Jake asked.

She took a breath and caught the musky scent of goat. Her panic spiked as cloven hooves clattered on the pavement behind her. Snarling, she twisted and looked up in time to see a huge fist launching straight at her.

The krampus walloped her face. The bones in her nose crunched like crushed potato chips, detonating pain inside her skull. The blow knocked her over, and the phone went flying. She crashed to the ground and landed in a heap on the pavement.

Head swimming, she rolled and attempted to stand. The whole world tilted at a crazy angle, and she followed it sideways. Hooves clomped toward her. Vision blurred, she stumbled, walking on the side of her feet.

The Rottweiler's furious barking rushed closer. He growled. A heavy thud, and then the dog released a high-pitched, piteous yelp. He made no further sounds.

"No." Victoria's heart wrenched for the poor dog. A sorrowful moan tore from her throat. Why hadn't he obeyed her?

Clomping again, moving closer. Scrambling, she shook her head. Her sight cleared enough for her to make out the beast's enormous form which loomed over her. A growl rumbled in her throat. She swung but missed, so her fist whizzed through empty air.

The krampus swooped in closer. His fist slammed into the side of her head.

The world went black.

CHAPTER 9

The throbbing in her head obliterated her ability to think. The pain became an excruciating pressure inside her skull that built and built. She moved with care, fearful the smallest movement would upset a delicate balance and burst her eyeballs. Groaning, Victoria pried open one eyelid to discover her body folded into a pretzel–her head bent forward, her knees jammed against her chest.

Cold iron bars crushed her on all sides. The confining cage was the right size to hold a child. She had no room to stand or maneuver. Thanks to her accelerated regeneration, her broken nose had already returned to its normal shape. The persistent headache told her not much time had passed. She healed fast.

As she raised her head, the bony fingers of a cramp

dug into her neck. A soft moan tore from her throat. Ignoring the pain, she struggled to rearrange her limbs. Eventually, she achieved a more comfortable position on her knees. She checked her pockets and confirmed her cell phone had been lost in the alley.

Victoria occupied the last cage, formerly empty, in the row of four. About ten feet away, she spotted a work-bench laden with sharp implements: knives, pokers, and even a pitch fork. Another steel drum full of ink stood beside the table. She didn't see the krampus.

To one side, a boy with a tear-streaked face watched her. The child stank of urine and feces. Her stomach heaved. She tried to keep all hints of anger from her face, lest she scare him. The boy's eyes were bloodshot, and chunks of dried snot clung to his skin. Even in his unkempt state, he looked like his mother.

"Are you Michael?" Victoria kept her voice soft.

Eyes widening, he stared at her and nodded. "How did you know?"

"Your mother is watching over you." Victoria wedged her fingers into the front pocket of her blue jeans and fished out the fire truck she had taken from the apart-ment. Twisting her arm, she pushed her hand through the bars and stretched far enough to offer Michael the toy.

After a moment's hesitation, he reached out his hand and took it from her. "The monster is going to kill me next," he said, staring at the truck. "It's already killed two other kids."

In the other two occupied cages, a male and a female watched them with wide, fearful eyes. The little girl looked about five years old. She pointed toward the drums full of black ink and spoke in a trembling voice. "The monster made them drown."

Victoria gagged on rage, hot fury blinding her reason. The children's fear evoked the protective instincts of her she-wolf. Her humanity dangled on a fragile thread. She clung to her self-control with stubborn determination and resisted the reflex to transform into a wolf. The last thing she wanted was to frighten the youngsters more.

Extending his slender arm between the bars, Michael turned his hand over, allowing the toy to fall from his grasp. He looked up to meet her puzzled gaze. "I stole it," he said with tears in his eyes. "I knew stealing was wrong, but I wanted a new toy. My mom's dead 'cause I'm bad. I deserve to be punished. The monster said so..."

Victoria's chest hurt from the effort of holding back a furious growl. Tears stung her eyes. Panting, she managed a semblance of calm. "It's a liar. Listen to me, Michael. It's a liar. You haven't done anything bad enough to deserve *this*."

"I'm scared." Lips trembling, he stared at her. Tears spilled down his cheeks.

"It's not going to hurt you. I'm going to kill it. I promise." She gripped the bars of the cage and tested their strength. The iron held, but her struggle sent her prison to rocking crazily on its chain.

Attracted by the sound of their voices, the krampus returned on clomping hooves. Tail lashing, he paused, and his attention centered upon Victoria's swinging cage. His red-rimmed eyes narrowed in clear annoyance. He had a dark aura, black at the center, tinted with dark red about the edges. With mincing steps, he approached her enclosure.

"You cannot escape," the krampus said in a lovely, flute-like voice. "The bars are enchanted."

Victoria scented doubt and desire emanating from him. She locked gazes with him and sneered. "It's easy to act brave while I'm behind these bars. The truth is you're a coward. A child thief who preys on innocents. Come here and see if you can handle someone who's not afraid of you, goat boy."

His eyes narrowed, and his tone grew angry. "Coward, I am not. It is my appointed task to punish wicked children. I am Krampus, the Yuletide Lord. The son of the Goddess Hel, descended of Loki the Trickster."

The krampus reached for her cage and caught the bars on either side. His hands were leathery, the backs covered in thick fur. His pointed nails clinked on the metal. He lowered his head so they faced each other. "My belly aches."

So did hers. A great, yawning emptiness. She craved goat with a ravenous hunger that made her mouth water. The closer he came, the more the beast smelled like prey.

"You eat guilt?" Victoria asked, seeking affirmation of what Jake Barrett had told her. The concept of a monster that fed on emotions struck her as preposterous. Easier said than believed... She stifled an inane giggle.

...thought the skeptical werewolf.

"Sin. Shame. Misery." His giggle embodied pure wickedness. He whispered to her in that honeyed falsetto. "My desire is for sweet children, my usual feast. Your guilt, so delicious, calls to me."

"You want me? Come and get me." Victoria beckoned with a provocative come-hither smile that disguised her disgust. She summoned her magic, allowing it to spill across her skin and spread, a sparking golden glow. As Freya's priestess, she understood passion. The krampus craved guilt, so she offered hers readily. She wallowed in the suffocating mire, offering up her shame and pain over Daniel's death as a sumptuous meal.

The krampus's pupils dilated. His mouth gaped, and he paused. "Do not know what you are. Stench like wet dog."

His hesitation worried her. She needed him to open the cage. Stifling panic, she focused on the awful self-recrimination she harbored in her heart. "Does it matter what I am?" she asked in a sultry voice. "Can't you sense how the guilt eats at me?"

"Yesss..." he hissed. A thick ruby-red tongue slid past his lips and flicked against the iron bars. Arousal turned his scent pungent. "I shall suck your soul, drain you dry. You shall sustain me for a long, long time."

With clumsy eagerness, he fumbled with the lock of her cage. It took him three tries to work the elaborate mechanism. The doors swung on concealed hinges and parted wide to either side. At last, she understood how her captor had gotten her into the confined space in the first place.

"I'm so tempting. Irresistible," she teased. Muscles rippled beneath her skin, her wolf straining to burst free of the confines of her human skin.

" Yesss..." His rough hands closed on her forearms. Sulfuric breath filled her nostrils, and she gagged, tasting bile in the back of her throat. In counterpoint to her nausea, her stomach growled. An immense aching emptiness in her sides.

His beaked nose thrust into her face, and she resisted the urge to bite off the bulbous tip. With an effort, Victoria stayed passive while he dragged her from the kennel. The children's whimpers and sobs were hardest to ignore. She had to make sure she was safely clear of the young ones before she acted.

"Show me how your lover died." With her dangling

from his grasp, the krampus straightened to his full height.

Shocked, she gasped. "How the hell do you know–"

"I know all about your sins," he said, cackling.

Their eyes locked, and a crude psychic tendril invaded her mind, burrowing deep, seeking her guilt. Caught off-guard, Victoria reeled under the unexpected assault. The beast before her vanished, and Daniel took his place. Reality fractured, blurred at the edges, and reformed.

Early December. She and Daniel had cleared out a nest of vampires from an abandoned gas station in the desert outside Phoenix. The building was little more than four walls supporting a rickety roof. All the windows were shattered. Broken fragments of glass littered the dirty floors. Looters had long ago taken anything worth having.

Daniel insisted on making a final sweep of the area. The prospect of spending more time with him pleased her, so she humored him.

"It's high noon. All of the vamps are gonna be in the ground. What exactly are you expecting to find?" Wielding a machete, Victoria assumed the lead. Broken glass crunched beneath her athletic shoes as she inspected rows of toppled shelving.

"You can never be too careful." Daniel offered her a cheeky grin. Then he changed the subject. "I have two weeks of vacation coming up over Christmas and the New Year..."

She stopped and swiveled to face him. His edgy stance and the charged streaks of aggression in his aura hinted that he was up to something. Her tension fed on his. "Do you have big plans?"

His even teeth slashed in a confident smile. "Cabo San Lucas, baby. Two weeks of sun and sand."

Her heart skipped. It took all her self-control not to squeal or jump up and down in excitement. She arched her brow. "You can have sun and sand in Arizona."

He grinned. "And surf."

She huffed. He had her there.

His chocolate brown eyes pinned her with deter-mined intensity, stealing her breath. "Come with me."

Unaccountably, she flushed and immediately felt ridiculous. They'd been lovers for almost a year. The man shouldn't be capable of reducing her to a stammering school girl. He might be a renowned hunter, but she was the daughter of Alpha wolves.

"I can't." She replied more brusquely than she liked and turned away to conceal her turmoil. More than anything, she wanted to cast off her responsibilities and run away with him. But she had obligations...

"Victoria." Daniel caught her wrist.

Behind her, a whip-like crack split the air. Daniel gurgled.

Jolted, Victoria spun. Her horrified mind registered the expression of absolute shock on Daniel's face. A serpentine length of muscle covered in barbs coiled about his throat, the hooks digging into his soft flesh. Blood flowed in a steady stream from his torn jugular.

He used both hands to pry the thing from his throat, and the bleeding sped. Bright red. Frantic, she reached for him, summoning her healing magic, but it was too little and too late to do any good.

In a matter of seconds, Daniel died in her arms. Wicked laughter danced around her, and she registered the macabre visage of a vampire. With a distant shock, she realized the barbed tentacle of flesh that had killed her lover was the thing's *tongue.*

A twisted alien thought filled her mind. *His death is your fault.*

"Yes." Victoria blinked back tears. She vividly recalled that monster's fucking tongue and how desperately she wished for a do-over. Given the opportunity, she would rip it out by the root.

The devil in her mind giggled. *You failed to protect him.*

Her wolf rumbled in anger. Victoria closed her eyes and then opened them again. The world around her flickered, and the krampus's beastly visage returned.

"Show me his death again." A thick ruby tongue snaked from the corner of his mouth and approached her face with a sinuous motion. The tip slapped against her cheek and licked toward her mouth. A trail of hot saliva trickled down her face.

A furious growl rumbled deep in her throat. She jerked her head to the side and allowed her wolf its freedom. The transformation burst over her with excruciating swiftness. Stretching her skin taut, the bones of her face distended and pushed into an elongated muzzle.

Snapping jaws, glistening canines.

In a blink, she caught the krampus's tongue between her teeth and bit clean through the offending appendage. Hot blood filled her mouth, and she swallowed the chunk of flesh whole. The meal hit her empty stomach as welcome warmth. Her sides clenched. She craved more.

Howling in agony, the krampus thrust her away. His bleeding tongue whipped back into his mouth, and his hand flew to cover the injury. She clung, digging her claws deep into his muscular arms and leaving bloody rents. Her jaws closed on his shoulder. He tasted like goat too. Salivating, she ripped another chunk of meat free and swallowed it whole. The arm meat was too sinewy, but she didn't mind. Goodness hit her stomach. Her first decent meal in a week.

She could acquire a taste for goat meat.

Backing away, he dragged her across the room. Victoria continued her transformation into a wolf, acquiring both height and weight. Bones broke and reformed. Her entire body underwent painful contortions as her torso and limbs lengthened and thickened. Her clothing stretched and then split. Her feet tore through her shoes. The remnants of fabric fell away, leaving her covered in snow-white fur.

In their cages, the children shrieked and sobbed in terror. She regretted frightening them further, but it couldn't be helped. She halted the change midway. Her bipedal form resembled the classic movie wolfman. The shape allowed her to use her wolf's strength and natural weaponry. She also retained the use of her hands and rudimentary speech.

The krampus stared at her in open astonishment. "What are you?"

Victoria smiled, displaying all her glistening white teeth. Saliva dripped from the tips. "The big bad wolf, come to gobble you up, Billy Goat Gruff."

A girl's scream rent the air. Her instincts to protect the youngsters kicked in, and she reflexively turned toward the sound. The fight had brought them perilously close to the cages, putting the children in peril. Bracing, she tugged on the devil and attempted to drag him away from the cages. He outweighed her by a lot, so she only moved him a few feet.

Bellowing, the krampus snarled and raked her, sharp nails gouging her arm. Despite her transformation, he was several feet taller than her. Taking advantage of the difference, he yanked her off her feet. He swung her around and slammed her into the closest wall.

Her side took the brunt of the brutal impact. Ribs snapped. The searing pain weakened her grip enough to allow the krampus to rip free. Grasping her leg, he hefted her overhead and spun her before letting go. Her shoulders and upper back collided with a wall of shelves. Victoria crashed to the floor amidst falling boxes and containers and lay in a stunned heap. A fog of pain enveloped her head.

A hoof rang on concrete. It struck once. Twice.

Victoria twisted and looked up just as the krampus lowered his head, preparing to charge. Those wicked-looking horns aimed straight at her. A startled *oh-shit* yelp escaped her. Adrenaline surging, she ignored her body's pained protest and rolled upright. Crouched on all fours, she readied to dodge.

His breath heaved with the power of a train engine, and the krampus charged straight at her. His hooves clattered like thunder, reverberating in the small room. Victoria waited until the last possible second and then stepped aside with a deft twist.

As she darted past, Victoria delivered a quick bite to his hindquarters. She aimed for his hamstrings, hoping to cripple him. She missed the vital tendons. Instead, her mouth closed on his hock and ripped a hunk free. Her mouth filled with raw flesh and hot blood. The thigh meat was tastier than his arms, rich but gamey. She swallowed the mouthful in a single gulp and went back for another bite, only to discover he'd already passed her. Her jaws closed on empty air.

Running at full speed, the krampus slammed into the same wall she had struck a minute before. The remaining intact shelves came crashing down. Remarkably, he remained upright, although the collision clearly disoriented him.

A burst of excited snarls and barks escaped her throat. Victoria leapt straight up and landed upon the devil's trunk. Her snapping jaws drove toward his throat. While he rose, she secured a bite hold and sank her teeth into the heavily-muscled flesh about his jugular. She pressed her body against his chest. Determined to hang on, she wrapped her limbs about his barrel torso and dug into his back with her claws.

The krampus roared and charged into another set of shelves. More debris rained about them. Clinging close, she nimbly avoided another blow. His failure to dislodge her added fervor to his escape attempts. They ran and twisted, colliding with pallets and knocking over a drum. Black fluid spilled everywhere, coating the floor. The moans and sobs of the imprisoned children edged her awareness. The entire time, her jaws remained locked on his throat, constricting his air supply. Inevitably, strangulation would weaken him enough so she could deal the death blow.

Panting for breath, the krampus ground to a halt and collapsed onto his knees. Victoria's feet finally touched the ground again. In a final act of desperation, he turned his great strength against her. His wickedly sharp nails raked her back. Her head swam with pain, and red clouded her vision.

The krampus sought softer flesh and positioned his hands just below her ribcage. He dug in with his nails, attempting to disembowel her. In self-defense, Victoria loosened her hold on his chest and blocked him with her elbows. She braced in anticipation of the crippling pain of a gut injury. Her jaws remained locked on his throat. She hung on with pit bull determination.

She'd sooner die than let go.

"They're over here!" a man's voice shouted. Heavy footsteps pounded, announcing their approach.

The hunters had arrived.

A distant note of hope edged her awareness, but it was far too soon to relax. Locked in a contest of pure strength versus strength, Victoria wrestled with the krampus,. She strained to gain the upper hand, but the beast was stronger than her. The exertion wrung a pained groan from the she-wolf. Her muscles burned, and her injuries ached.

When Jake Barrett and Skinner entered the area, relief flooded her. She'd never been so damn happy to see an enemy in her entire life.

"Victoria, let go on my mark," Jake ordered with the

authority of a man accustomed to being obeyed. Hefting a heavy chain, the hunter attacked the krampus from the rear. He dropped the length over the beast's head.

At the same moment, Victoria opened her jaws and dropped to the floor. She landed flat on her back. Momentarily freed, the krampus swallowed a huge draught of fresh air. He lurched, and one of his hooves struck her elbow. A painful jolt shot through the joint.

The hunter secured another loop of chain about the beast's throat. Strangled again, the krampus bucked, trying to throw Jake from his back.

Growling, Victoria rolled away to avoid being trampled. Over the krampus's head, she shot Jake a nasty glare. "You're late."

The Hunter King's grimace bore a powerful resemblance to a grin. The muscles in his arms and shoulders bulged as he hauled back on the chains. The dagger tattoo on his forearm glowed red hot, pulsating as though impatient to taste blood.

She couldn't understand why he hadn't drawn it.

"You started without me," Jake said.

"I got bored." Victoria circled the krampus, watching for an opening. The chain pricked her curiosity. She wondered why they were trying to capture it. Why hadn't they just killed it?

Taking up the slack in the chain, Jake tossed one end to Skinner. Working together, the men tightened the noose taut about the krampus's throat. Bellowing his rage, the krampus surged to his feet with renewed resistance.

"Over the pipes!" Jake tossed his length of chain into the air and over the exposed piping mounted to the ceiling. As soon as the ligature dropped, he grabbed the end and applied his entire weight as an anchor.

"Got it!" Skinner heaved his end of the chain toward the ceiling, but his throw fell short. His side of the restraint went slack.

Head lowered, the krampus swung toward Skinner. His horn caught the human in the shoulder. The pointed end punched clean through, and the tip appeared out the hunter's back. A terrible shout tore from him, and he grabbed the horn at the base with both hands.

Jake hauled the chain in an attempt to control the beast. For a second, the additional leverage allowed him to restrain the krampus on his own. Then the chain links slid on the pipe, and the loose end rose.

The krampus reared to his full height, hefting the injured hunter on his horn. A shake of his massive head sent Skinner careening through the air. The thrown man smacked into the far wall and slid to the floor.

"Skinner!" Jake circled, attempting to reach his friend's side, but the krampus stood between them. At long last, the Hunter King drew his magical dagger. The tattoo weapon vanished from his forearm and appeared in his hand.

Unwilling to be left out of the fight, Victoria flanked the krampus's other side, seeking an opening. With that weapon in Jake's hand, she preferred not to get too close. The damn thing sent shivers down her spine. Legend said the weapon couldn't be sheathed until Jake had taken a life.

She'd asked Daniel about it once. He'd laughed. *"I asked the same thing when I was six. All dad did was smile."*

Twisting and shoving, the beast shrugged off the chain about his neck. Lowering his head, the krampus brandished his horns and stomped his hooves. He menaced another charge. Hot breath flew from flared nostrils. Blood soaked the wiry black hair of his massive chest and hock where she'd bitten. Despite the injuries, the creature presented a formidable threat.

She wanted to kill the krampus so bad she could taste it.

Roaring, she rushed toward him. The krampus swung toward her voice. She took three running steps and leapt straight at the beast's head. With both hands, she caught hold of his horns and used her strength to force his head down.

Snorting, the krampus jerked away from her. His back hit the wall, and for once the close quarters worked to her advantage. While the beast thrashed from side to side, she held on for all she was worth. One of his horns was slick with blood, making it difficult to keep a good grip. A steady snarl reverberated in her throat, escaping in bursts as she panted for breath.

Jake rushed in, his burning dagger held aloft.

"Kill it." Victoria grated from the side of her mouth. She pulled on his horns to straighten his neck and strove to hold him steady.

"With pleasure." Jake brought the knife overhead in a wide arc. The molten blade struck the back of the devil's neck and cleaved through the spine. The blow severed the backbone, exposing muscle and bone, but failed to decapitate the beast. Blood poured from the wound. The sound of sizzling accompanied the odor of burnt flesh.

Caught in his death throes, the krampus wailed and lurched to the side. Victoria kept him upright. The scent of fresh meat flooded her nostrils, tempting her wolf. Her mouth watered, and hunger clawed at her sides. Through an act of will, she quashed the impulse to fall on the drying beast and gorge.

Jake grunted and yanked his blade free of the beast's back. When he swung the knife again, an arc of blood sprayed from the blade. The weapon hit straight on the mark and sliced clean through the krampus's neck. The body dropped to the floor, leaving Victoria holding the head by the horns. A fountain of blood flowed from the body, forming a puddle. The dark red fluid saturated the white fur of her feet.

Tilting her head, Victoria looked down into the krampus's face. Red-rimmed eyes bright with malice stared up at her and then dimmed to black coals. Her mouth curled into a sneer of disgust. She opened her hands and dropkicked the head, sending it flying across the room.

Abruptly, her awareness of her injuries hit her like a freight train. Panting, she dropped to a crouch and sat on her heels. Oh, how she hurt. Even with her accelerated healing, it promised to be hours before she felt one-hundred percent again.

Gritting her teeth, she initiated the painful change from her half-wolf form to human. Her face and hands returned to normal first, then the rest of her followed. Her fur retracted into her flesh. Bones snapped and knit. Transformation sped her healing, repairing some but not all the damage.

Fully human, she knelt naked in the pool of krampus blood. She looked up and found Jake Barrett standing over her, the burning dagger poised. As their gazes met, his hand clenched about the hilt. Muscles rippled beneath his scarred skin and traveled the length of his arm. In that moment, she fully expected the blade to descend and take her head.

Daniel had inherited his brown eyes from his father. Jake's had crow's feet at the corners, and his soul was infinitely more cynical. His face set in a stoic mask, but his discipline had cracks. She read the hesitation, the temptation, as he wrestled with the instinct to kill her.

"You're not afraid of death," Jake said.

"No, why should I be? My soul belongs to Freya." Victoria's first death had been the result of combat, in service to her goddess, who had returned her to life to serve as Valkyrie.

A tug pulled on the corner of his mouth. Those ferocious eyes burned. "You should be afraid of me."

"Oh, I am." The man terrified her, but she refused to be cowed. She tilted her head to the side, exposing her throat. Her tone turned taunting and provocative. "Kill me and you'll never have your answers about how Daniel died."

Suffering distorted Jake's face, and his mouth contorted into a grimace. "Our deal stands. On your honor."

"On my honor." Victoria agreed without hesitation. "When Jasper and my pack go free, I'll surrender my life to you."

"I asked for answers," he said sourly. A severe expression replaced his agony, and he gave a curt nod. The burning dagger vanished from his hand. The tattoo appeared on his arm. "Agreed."

His choice of words gave her the faintest hope. Maybe he'd actually allow her to explain about Daniel's death. At the same time, she rejected the possibility. Listening and granting clemency were two separate things. How could she ask Jake Barrett to show her mercy when she couldn't forgive herself?

Victoria straightened and stepped out of the puddle. Her bare feet left bloody tracks on the concrete. Her nudity caused her no shame or embarrassment. Few shifters were shy.

Jake averted his eyes. Without a word, he removed his shirt and tossed it to her. "Here."

Swallowing a snicker, Victoria caught the garment out of the air and pulled it over her head. The cloth was damp with perspiration and smelled like Jake Barrett. The hem hung past her knees, but it was better than nothing.

Across the room, Skinner moaned.

Victoria and Jake turned in unison toward the injured man. The fallen hunter struggled to sit upright. Sweat glistened on his brown skin, and blood stained the front of his torn shirt.

Jake rushed to his friend, dropped to one knee, and placed a hand on Skinner's uninjured shoulder. "You're injured."

Grunting, Skinner persisted. "No shit, Sherlock."

"This ain't the time. Stay down." Leaning over, Jake made his point by pinning the injured man.

Skinner offered brief, fierce resistance. Then he collapsed, cursing up a storm.

Across the room, Victoria hesitated, torn between offering to help and keeping a safe distance. As a nurse and a healer, her instincts called her to tend to the injured. Common sense kept her silent. The hunter was her enemy. She owed him nothing.

Instead, she hurried to the imprisoned children. Michael and the girl were bravely quiet. Piteous sobs wracked the smallest of the three, a little boy who appeared to be about three. If these were the same abducted children mentioned in the newspaper article, then the girl's name was Crystal. The youngest boy should be Vincent.

"Is it dead?" Michael asked.

"Yes, it's dead," Victoria assured him. "Give me a sec, and I'll get you out of there." She stopped, staring up. Ceiling-mounted chains supported the cages, placing the locks well out of her reach. A burst of annoyance washed over her, and she swallowed a word inappropriate for young ears.

"Stand on a barrel," Michael said.

Victoria's mouth twisted into a wry smile. "Good idea." She grabbed the empty steel drum that had been tipped over during the fight and dragged it toward the enclosures. Once she stood it on end, it served as an excellent makeshift ladder.

She positioned it before Michael's cage first. Victoria fumbled with the locking mechanism which involved interlocking tumblers and finger placement. After a few minutes, she got the correct combination. The lock snapped open, and she pulled the doors wide.

With a cry, Michael flew into her open arms. She hugged the small boy close and stroked the back of his head. He stank of filth and fear, but she didn't care. "Shh, it's okay, Michael. Your mother loves you. She sent me to save you."

"My mother is dead," Michael said. "I saw the monster kill her."

"Her spirit is watching over you." Victoria lowered him to the ground. "No matter what happens, always remember that, okay?"

The child nodded. "I know."

"Hang tight, buddy. I'm going to get the other kids free, okay?"

Michael dipped his chin. "I'll be okay."

Victoria's heart ached for him. The poor boy had no living family to return home to. He would probably wind up as a ward of the state and faced placement in foster care. She wished there were something more she could do for him, but it was out of her hands. She already had more people depending on her than she could protect.

"What's your name, sweetie?" Victoria freed the little

girl next and lowered her gently to the ground. The child's glassy eyes worried her.

The girl's stare remained blank for a long moment, then she blinked and said, "Crystal."

"Crystal, stay with Michael. You're going to be okay."

Unbidden, Michael approached and took Crystal's hand in his own, freeing Victoria to deal with the final cage. Opening the doors, she pulled out a boy no older than three. "Vincent, let me help you out of there."

The little one sobbed and clung to her but never spoke a word. Cradling the toddler against her chest, Victoria jumped down from the barrel. She landed squarely on both feet.

Movement caught her peripheral vision. Victoria turned and found Jake standing close–too close for comfort. Clutching the boy tighter, she took a quick step backward. The hunter possessed uncanny stealth, another trait he shared with his son. Few people were able to sneak up on her.

The man's features remained set in an unreadable mask. He studied the boy in her arms and then his gaze swept over the other two children. Michael and Crystal held hands, clinging to each other. Jake's clenched hands betrayed his inner turmoil, alluding to a tightly constrained anger.

Victoria perceived sympathy and horror in his familiar brown eyes. For about the hundredth time, she reminded herself that he was the enemy, no longer her ally. She moved closer to the children and hovered protectively over them. Stepping forward, she laid her hand upon Michael's shoulder.

Jake's gaze strayed to the cages, and his horror intensified. Upon seeing the conditions the children had been kept in, he swore, "Son of a—"

"Language!" Her blue eyes narrowed, and she shot him a warning look over the top of the toddler's head. Her breath hissed between her teeth.

"Beach," Jake finished lamely. Despite his reputation as a merciless killer, the hunter had a sense of decency.

She smiled. Daniel's compassion and humanity were one of the things she'd loved best... *Shit.* She squeezed her eyes closed against a sudden onslaught of sorrow. She really needed to get a fucking grip and stop comparing Jake Barrett to his dead son.

"We need to get the children out of here," Victoria said, casting a glance toward the krampus's decapitated body. Where had that head gone?

"I agree." Jake spread his arms, herding Michael and Crystal before him. "Take them outside and tell them to wait. Then come back in. Skinner's hurt pretty bad. I've stopped the bleeding and stabilized him for the moment, but he needs a healer."

Victoria's expression hardened. "Why the hell would I heal him?"

Jake's jaw worked. His voice was flat, devoid of emotion. "It'll go easier on you if you cooperate. Skinner is my best man, and I owe him. One way or another, you're going to help him."

Victoria's heart palpitated. Shit. His lack of intonation scared her worse than any amount of shouting could have. How did the man manage to pack so much threat into such a monotone statement? At the same time, she found his choice of words interesting. Why was Skinner his best man, and not his second son, Sawyer?

She stared at her enemy. She actually preferred to help over allowing a man to die, though it wasn't like he was offering her many options. She shrugged. "Fine, I'll do what I can."

"You do that."

Victoria offered Michael her hand and addressed the children, "I want you all to close your eyes. I'll lead you outside."

Michael's gaze darted toward the decapitated corpse they had to pass on their way out. His throat worked as he swallowed. His scent was thick with fear, but he held fast to his courage. He accepted Victoria's hand and clung to Crystal.

"Okay," Michael said. "Let's go."

Victoria's heart swelled with fierce pride at his courage. The children closed their eyes. They continued to hold hands while she escorted them into the alley. A black SUV, presumably Jake's, was parked just outside the rear entrance. She located her mobile phone on the ground, stooped to pick it up, and started to slip it into a pocket. Only to realize she wasn't wearing jeans. Sighing, she settled for holding it.

"I need for you to wait here. I have to go back inside because a man is hurt." Bending, Victoria passed the toddler to Crystal. The girl sat on the ground with her back against the wall and hugged the boy.

The kids stared at her with fearful round eyes. Michael said, "Don't leave us alone."

Victoria sighed and searched for the right words. If Jake was right about Skinner's condition, she didn't have much time. Yet, she was loath to rush off and leave the children unprotected.

An anxiety-ridden bark interrupted whatever she'd been about to say. Startled, Victoria scanned the alley. Blessed relief filled her when she spotted the Rottweiler crouched between two trash bins. She'd thought the krampus had killed him. She whistled softly and patted her knee, issuing a summons.

The Rottweiler whimpered. He rose and trotted forward, his head and tail lowered in a show of submission. The children regarded the animal with open curiosity and no fear. Victoria extended her hand, and the dog pushed his muzzle into her palm, licking her fingers.

She caressed the dog's soft ears and leaned forward to whisper to him. "You're to stay with these children and protect them. Do you understand?"

The dog's stubby tail wagged. Lifting her hand, Victoria urged the youngsters closer so they could touch him. "Michael, this is my friend. Go ahead and pet him."

Michael hesitated, staring suspiciously at the dog. The other two children huddled behind him. His shaking hand rose slightly. "What's his name?"

"He doesn't have one. He doesn't have an owner." A situation she desperately hoped was about to change. The dog and the boy both needed someone.

"I've always wanted a dog." Michael was the first to approach, extending a nervous hand to stroke the Rottweiler's head. The dog's stubby tail wagged furiously, and the boy's confidence soared.

"See, he likes you," Victoria murmured.

Within seconds, a smile blossomed on Michael's face. "I'm going to call him Rascal."

Her throat closed, and her heart ached. Her voice emerged as a dry rasp. "That's a good name."

The other two children followed his lead, and soon enough all three kids were crowded around the dog. She waited for a couple moments while they became acquainted.

"I have to go inside," she said again. "But Rascal is going to watch over you. Will that be okay?"

Michael looked up and squared his shoulders. "We'll be okay."

She took a couple of steps, then hesitated. "I'll be right inside if you need me."

The boy looked at her. "Go on," he said, putting his forehead against the dog's. "I've got this."

Grinning, she turned back and almost walked straight into the mountain that was Jake Barrett. Eyes flashing, she pulled up. "Stop doing that!"

He chuckled. "Pay more attention. Where did the mutt come from?"

"The 'mutt' helped me find this place. Without him, we couldn't have rescued the children." Victoria's tone slipped toward testy. She disliked the implied slur against the dog.

A grunt served as Jake's reply.

Her impatience ratcheted another notch higher. Didn't the man have even the remotest sense of urgency? It was his injured friend, not hers, who awaited their return.

He cleared his throat. "I got to thinking. The little ones shouldn't have to sit on wet pavement in the cold. They can wait in my car."

"Oh." She huffed. His thoughtfulness took the wind right out of her sails. Under the pretext of helping Crystal and the toddler to rise, Victoria averted her gaze.

Jake opened the rear door, and they placed the two children into the back seat.

"Michael, come on." Victoria beckoned to the boy.

Michael's arms tightened about the dog's neck. "Not without Rascal."

A pleased smile tugged at her lips. She did her best to hide her smirk and failed in a spectacular way. She looked to Jake, one eyebrow arched in a silent question. Michael also turned his attention to the hunter.

"Damn mutt probably has fleas." Grumbling, Jake assisted Michael and the dog into the backseat and closed the door. He circled to the back and opened the tailgate. When he returned, he had on a fresh shirt.

She experienced a twinge of envy and wished she'd had the sense to bring a change of clothing. Typically, she had a go-bag for the occasions when she would have to shift. But in the excitement, the duffle had gotten left in the back of the pickup truck.

Jake addressed Victoria. "Let's get back inside."

She nodded and led the way.

Skinner lay on his back atop a wooden pallet that got him off the wet concrete floor. A waded leather jacket pillowed his head, and the discarded remains of a small first aid kit littered the area.

At a glance, Skinner appeared to be unconscious. Probably in shock. Victoria knelt beside him to confirm, checking his vitals. His breathing was shallow and his complexion pallid due to blood loss . His heart labored in his chest, each beat a valiant struggle for life.

"You did a decent patch job," she said, inspecting the injury. Gauze bandages swathed the hunter's shoulder.

"I've had a lot of practice," Jake said grimly. He knelt beside his friend. His tone reminded her that the hunters didn't have healers. They relied on traditional medicine.

Their dangerous chosen profession made them no strangers to injury and death.

She nodded absently and peeled away the wrappings. Her hands were steady even though she inwardly balked at the filthy conditions. The busy work settled her anxiety and provided a convenient, albeit short-lived, reprieve. She faced a dilemma. As a rule, her people did *not* use their gifts to benefit outsiders.

Composing her thoughts, she opened herself in prayer. She reached for a spiritual connection with her goddess. *My Lady? I need you. I have a big problem.*

Freya's warmth touched her. *I've been watching.*

Any advice? Victoria removed the last of the bindings.

Do you want advice or approval, Priestess?

"Either," Victoria muttered. "Both."

Across from her, Jake Barrett frowned. Those penetrating eyes locked on her face, and the man gave the impression of uncanny awareness. As if he could hear their entire conversation.

Spooked, Victoria shuddered and dismissed the possibility. Her overactive imagination always got the better of her. Mouth open, Victoria lowered her face closer to Skinner's shoulder and inhaled his scent. Her wolf surfaced. Golden light spilled from her eyes, but her transformation progressed no further.

Bracing, she summoned her healing magic. A soft halo

emanated from her palms. The moment her fingers touched his bare skin, Skinner's life pattern lit up. She perceived the lacerations to flesh and muscle, internal bleeding, and shattered bones. He had lost an enormous amount of blood, and his body was in shock.

"He's dying." Her mouth turned down at the corners. "I'm not sure I can save him."

"I once saw your mother heal a man who'd been all but cut in half," Jake said. "She brought your father back from the dead."

Victoria cut him off. "I'm not my mother. My skills as a healer are minimal. I can mend cuts and bruises—"

"You help him!" Jake's eyes narrowed, and his fists rose even as his volume dropped to a dangerous low. He left the *or else* hanging, but the implied threat was clear.

Distressed, Victoria reached again for Freya. *Goddess? Please? Do I have your permission to do this?*

You didn't seek my permission when you attempted to heal Daniel.

Taken aback, Victoria blinked. Her mouth opened. No sound emerged. Freya hadn't brought up Victoria's failed attempts to heal Daniel before he'd died. Not once in the last couple of weeks, not even a hint of disapproval or reprimand. Belatedly, she realized she should have sought permission. Bittersweet acknowledgement prevented her from apologizing.

She'd do so all over again in a heartbeat.

Freya sighed. *Do what you must. Know this: I cannot heal him for you.*

I understand. Thank you, Goddess. Unshed tears stung her eyes. She lowered her face to hide her sorrow. The light flowing from her hands intensified, illuminating the man's injury. She extended her power and joined her soul to Skinner's. Concentrating, she drew his life pattern into synchronization with her own. Her steady heartbeat stabilized his erratic pulse.

Even unconscious, the stubborn human fought her. He resisted her efforts to impose spiritual and physical harmony between them. Skinner gasped, and his entire body convulsed while he fought to shake off her touch. She employed her superior strength to hold him down so his struggles would not worsen the wound. Without the direct support of Freya or her pack, there was no margin for error.

Damn it, she hated asking for help, but she had no other options. Scowling, Victoria extended an open hand toward Jake. "You know how this works. I'm already drained from the fight with the krampus, and my pack isn't here to help me."

"Fuck that." Jake held back. Distrust tainted his scent. Negative sentiment streaked his aura.

"He's your friend," Victoria said. "Do you want him to live?"

The Hunter King was a storm about to rage. A fierce, brief battle waged across his countenance. In the end, loyalty won over hatred. He spat out a curse and grabbed hold of her hand, enveloping it within his callused grip.

The moment they touched, Victoria reached for his power, seeking to forge a temporary bond between them. Under normal circumstances, she would have refused to even attempt it. The man was human and her enemy. This situation, however, was desperate. Besides, she doubted the connection could survive so much animosity for long.

The force of his personality knocked her off kilter. Victoria gasped and almost dropped the fragile spell bridging their souls. For a human, Jake Barrett possessed a staggering amount of personal power. It was widely known the hunter commanded powerful magic, but he craftily concealed the true extent. Through some arcane art, not just hundreds, but thousands of men were mystically bound to him. Superficially, their connection resembled the pack bond in underlying structure. She'd have loved to explore it further. Even if she had that ability, there was no time.

Tuning out the others, she concentrated on the Hunter King. At the center of his soul, she encountered a core of pure pain, agonizing sorrow for the death of his son... and so much anger. She hurt for him and with him, and yet she wanted nothing more than to rip his beating heart from his breast. He had killed her parents and many members of her pack.

A good man, but also a vengeful man.

She must never forget. Tears stung her eyes, and her throat closed. Through an act of will, Victoria shoved her personal feelings down deep and sealed them behind a wall. Instead of turning from Jake Barrett's hatred, she embraced it. She summoned and channeled the dark emotions, transforming them into healing energy.

Victoria mapped out the major severed blood vessels and halted the internal bleeding. She repaired the most vital veins and arteries first. Then she strengthened the bone in his shattered shoulder blade. Her technique was crude. If he lived, he would still require medical attention.

Too quickly, she depleted her reserves, leaving her weakened. Jake's true potential remained almost untapped, and that frightened her worse than ever before. The Hunter King wasn't a mere mortal, and she wasn't sure she wanted to know more about him.

Gasping, Victoria let go of Jake's hand and severed the bond uniting them. She maintained her connection to Skinner long enough to verify he would live. For magical healing, her work qualified as battle field triage. She had done what was necessary to keep the man alive until he could receive proper treatment.

She removed her hands from Skinner's chest and allowed the magic to dissipate. "He'll live, for now. You need to get him to a doctor," she said, looking at Jake. "I couldn't fix everything."

The man's expression was unreadable. He stared at her with hard eyes and nodded. "Those children need to be taken to safety too. We'll take them in and then we'll go get your boy."

Balking, Victoria shot to her feet. "No. No way. I'm not walking into an area full of your men and getting shot on sight."

Clenched jaws and gleaming eyes signaled the return of his anger. "My men will obey me."

She snorted. "But your son won't, will he? I'll bet my canines that Sawyer isn't here now because he'd as soon kill me as look at me. You want me alive to answer your questions, but he just wants me dead."

The last time she had come face to face with Sawyer, he had opened fire on a street crowded with innocent people. The time before that, he had lobbed a hand grenade at her. She didn't expect his next reception to be any warmer. In her heart, she preferred to avoid him at all costs. Not because she feared him. She simply didn't want to be the one to murder Daniel's brother.

Jake's nostrils flared. "Sawyer is convinced you murdered Daniel in cold blood. Me..."

Her heart leapt at the unexpected ray of hope. If Jake Barrett was willing to listen, then perhaps she could explain Daniel's death. Maybe peace could be restored, maybe no one else needed to die.

"But you?" Victoria imposed blankness on her face, desperate not to reveal too much. She couldn't afford to show her cards. Not while Jasper remained a hostage to the hunters.

"I have my doubts."

Victoria exhaled. Oh yeah, dangerous, seductive hope. She dared not let down her guard around this man. "What will happen to the children?"

"For tonight, I'll take them to one of my people. We'll get them cleaned up and fed. You don't need to worry. We'll keep them safe until we can take them home."

"How do you intend to reunite them with their parents?" Much like her, young Michael had no one to go home to.

"I have friends in law enforcement," Jake said. "We'll keep this out of the press. If the children have families, I'll see to it they're reunited. If not, they won't wind up in the system. There are families willing to take in orphans."

She frowned. "They'd be raised by hunters."

His teeth flashed in a fierce grin. "Better than being raised by wolves."

Victoria's frown morphed to a glare. "So you say."

"At least they'd have adults around them who will understand the nature of their trauma," Jake said. "Adults who know monsters are real. These kids are gonna suffer from nightmares for the rest of their lives."

The man had the right of it.

She preferred to let the matter drop. "Okay."

"I'll drop Skinner at the hospital and get the children to safety," Jake said. "I'll meet you back here with the boy. Don't do anything stupid, like calling your pack."

"I won't," Victoria had already considered and rejected the idea of calling for help. Rand and the others would refuse to give her up without a fight. Another confrontation with the hunters would likely get the rest of her people killed.

With any luck, the others were well on the way to Santa Fe. Still, she worried about them. They hadn't responded to her distress while she battled the krampus. They were either too far away or experiencing troubles of their own.

Too weary for further discussion, she helped Jake move Skinner into the front passenger seat of his vehicle. Offering assurances, she buckled the three children into the back seat. Sorrow closed like a hand on her throat. She barely managed to bid them goodbye without crying.

Following Jake, she circled to the front of the vehicle. "When will you be back?"

"I'll be an hour." Jake regarded her with hard eyes.

Victoria didn't look away from the man's relentless stare. Her lips pulled back to reveal her teeth. "So help me, if you've harmed a hair on Jasper's head, I'll drag your soul to hell and pitch you in head first."

"Understood." The corner of his mouth tugged in what might have been a reluctant smile, but he turned away too soon.

While she watched, he climbed into the vehicle to take the children, the stray dog, and his injured friend to safety. Over the steering wheel, their gazes locked in a final unsettling stare before he drove away. Afterward, she blew out a breath she hadn't known was held.

For an hour, Victoria paced the perimeter of the parking lot. Time ticked past, one excruciating minute after another. The rain resumed, falling in a heavy downpour, and she took shelter against the side of the building beneath an overhang. After a couple minutes, a steady waterfall poured over the eaves.

As she waited, the tempest worsened. Legs of lightning supported the angry thunderclaps as they marched east. Victoria worried her lower lip, struggling to evade the bittersweet press of memories. No matter how hard she tried, the past remained inescapable and ever-present. The harder she tried not to think about Daniel, the more he occupied her thoughts.

Everything reminded her of him, especially storms.

Daniel had loved the spectacular lightning squalls that lit up the Arizona desert during the summer months. In defiance of safety and common sense, he always rushed outside and turned his face toward the sky. Wearing a maddened grin, he stood there until the wind blasted his hair back and water slicked it against his skull.

Despite her fears and reluctance, Daniel had chased her long and hard. Months slipped past, and his persistence gradually wore down her resistance. As summer turned into fall, they spent more and more time together. They retreated to the desert, far from the prying eyes of the people who would have disapproved.

"The thing I love best about Arizona is the sunsets," Victoria mused with a smile. Glorious strips of orange and red streaked the horizon just above the mountains to the west. Higher in the sky, purple clouds formed a wavy weave. A forceful wind blew from the east, and sturdy Saguaro cacti raised their thick arms in defiance. Dark storm clouds roiled in the east–a brooding monsoon moving off the Gulf of Mexico. In August, the remarkable storms arrived regularly in the late afternoon to early evenings.

She and Daniel lay side by side stretched out across the hood of the Chevelle. The heated metal warmed her back, and the muscular bicep of the man beside her served as a solid headrest. Contented, she wallowed in the fragile, fleeting wink of happiness. Perfect moments carried a momentous value that few people understood or properly cherished.

"Look at that!" Daniel jerked upright and flung his arm toward the east where bright lancing bolts arced from the sky to strike the ground below.

Disgruntled at losing her pillow, she sat up. "It's just another thunderstorm."

Miles distant, the vista lit with a lightning flash. Thunder followed in a lazy roll, a deep percussion booming. Victoria scented the air but smelled more windborne dust than moisture. She doubted the tempest carried much rain in its wide arms.

"It's more than that." Grinning, Daniel captured her wrist and dragged her hand toward him. He positioned her palm over his heart. "Do you feel that?"

Strong. Throbbing. Passion. Power.

The essence of the man.

She nodded her head, convinced she did indeed understand. He stole her breath much as he'd stolen her heart. To protect herself, she fostered an easy smile and twisted to glance over her shoulder. "We'd better put the top up."

His hand caught the side of her head, fingers spread wide and points positioned behind her ear, pinky tucked beneath her jaw. He captured her gaze. "The thing I love best about Arizona is you."

Her grin faltered. So much raw determination in his chocolate brown eyes. Always one to do things the difficult way, Victoria challenged him. "Only in Arizona?"

"Always. Forever." He leaned in and kissed her. Claimed her.

Their lips parted. She exhaled on his indrawn breath. "I love you too."

Fuck. Victoria ripped her mind from the reverie and took a shaky step. She forced her clenched fists to open. Sucking down a soggy breath, she abandoned the shelter of the eaves and walked into the rain. Droplets struck her face and washed away her tears.

Desperate for a distraction, she checked the time. An hour and a half since Jake had left. She wondered where he was, and her imagination conjured all sorts of awful scenarios for why he hadn't returned yet. Finally, she couldn't take the not knowing anymore. Abandoning her resolution not to contact her pack, she gripped her phone and made the call.

Sylvie answered on the first ring. Her tight voice conveyed distress tempered by relief. "Thank the goddess, Victory. Where have you been? Do you have Jasper? We've been worried sick waiting for you to call."

She smiled at the welcome sound of her friend's voice. "I'm fine. I don't have Jasper yet, but we slayed the monster and saved the kidnapped children. Is Rand okay?"

"Still as ornery as ever." A telltale pause followed, and then Sylvie asked, *"We?"*

"Jake Barrett."

The Skald groaned. "I suppose it's a blessing you're still alive."

"I'm working on getting Jasper back." Victoria infused her voice with confidence she didn't really feel. "Where are you?"

"We're on the northern outskirts of town," Sylvie said. "We couldn't go any farther without losing all the bars on the phone."

"The plan hasn't changed," Victoria said. "Wait there until dawn. If Jasper and I aren't back by sunrise, then head north to Santa Fe." Her voice caught in her throat. "Sylvie..."

Sylvie's voice grew tight. "What is it, Victory?"

"If I'm not back with Jasper, then you're to keep going. Don't allow Rand to come after me, even if you have to club him over the head. As your Alpha, that's an order. Do you understand me?"

The silence bristled with disapproval, but Sylvie gave a clipped reply. "I understand."

"Goddess watch over us," Victoria said, sending a quick prayer to Freya.

Sounding displeased, Sylvie echoed her words. "Goddess watch over you, Victoria Storm."

They ended the call.

She checked the clock on her phone and saw the hunter had been gone almost an hour and forty-five minutes. Her wolf roiled with turmoil. Her teeth sank into her lower lip, breaking skin, and she tasted the saltiness of blood on her tongue. Her instincts screamed something was wrong. She felt it in her gut.

Using her phone's call log, Victoria located Jake Barrett's number and hit dial. It rang twice before he answered.

"Hold on a second." His heavy breathing indicated physical exertion. In the background, she heard men shouting. And Jasper's voice, full of fear and anger, rose in a yell, but his words were unrecognizable.

"Barrett, what the hell is going on?" Fear crawled along the length of her spine, digging in with bony fingers. Dread pooled in her stomach.

Jake shouted over Victoria's demands. "No, lower your weapons."

"Damn it, Barrett, tell me—" Victoria's hands shook, and she feared her grip would crush the cell phone. She couldn't stand still. In desperation, she raced across the parking lot, running without direction.

The blast of a shotgun deafened her.

Victoria stumbled and stopped. Through the pack bond, she experienced Jasper's death as a blow to the heart, a severed limb, the demise of a soul. Shattered, an agonized howl tore from her throat, and she fell to her knees on the black pavement of the lot. Her cry of loss and sorrow rose above the din of city sounds, soaring into the night.

Jasper dead. How? Why?

Her pack experienced the boy's death also. Through their spiritual connection, she sensed her pack mates. She felt their rage and sorrow and heard their mourning howls even though they were miles distant, beyond the range of sound. When a child was lost, they all suffered.

Victoria's howl ended on a gasp. Tears streamed down her cheeks. Sucking air into her starved lungs, she brought the phone to her face.

"Why?" she asked, croaking the question.

"He wasn't supposed to get hurt." Disbelief colored Jake's voice.

Rage. Cruel, vicious rage crashed through her heart, blinding her to all else. She hissed. "You're the same as that krampus, Jake Barrett, a child thief who murders innocents. If it's the last thing I do, I'll make you pay. I swear to my goddess and on my honor as a Valkyrie. I'll have revenge."

Before he replied, she hurled the phone at the side of the building with all her immense strength. The device exploded into a hundred pieces. In that moment, she would have gladly ripped every member of the Barrett family to bloody shreds. She settled for destroying Jake's shirt instead.

Tears streaked her cheeks, but hatred defined her existence. The primal energy fueled her transformation to a wolf, shedding her human form and her humanity. Tilting her muzzle toward the moon, she roared her fury. In her heart, she committed to bloody, awful vengeance.

The voice of her goddess broke through her rage. Freya's silken contralto filled her mind, imposing inner peace. *Abide, Victoria. Jasper gave his life for you. He refused to allow your sacrifice.*

Victoria hesitated. Pleading, she asked, *Goddess, why would he kill Jasper? I was going to give myself up. I gave my word. He accepted it.*

Jasper tried to escape, and they murdered him. His soul is lost to us. He has gone to Niflheim, Hel's domain. He is damned.

Oh, Goddess. Please. No. Whimpering, the white wolf crouched close to the ground. In the gloomy underworld, Jasper's soul would suffer unspeakable torment. No worse fate could have befallen him.

Freya's golden voice filled her mind, drowning out all else, even thoughts of revenge. *Run, My Priestess. Run. For the sake of your pack, run. They need you. Death awaits you if you confront the hunters now.*

I'll avenge him. If it's the last thing I ever do. I'll avenge

Daniel, my parents, my pack. Everyone. A broken woman, she staggered to her feet and took an unsteady step.

To exact revenge for this cruelty would break you, Victoria. For the sake of your pack, for those who love you and whom you love, run.

I pledge my soul to revenge. Victoria swore to her goddess. *On my honor, and my family's name. I'll have a Valkyrie's vengeance.*

Freya's voice grew assertive. *Swear to seek justice, not revenge, and I shall witness your oath.*

She balked, desiring to argue. Then she stopped. In that moment, she didn't see any difference between revenge and justice. One way or another, the result was the same. So what did it matter which she swore to?

She chose the right words to receive her goddess's blessing while committing to revenge in her heart. *I swear to seek justice. On my honor, and my family's name.*

Blinding light destroyed Victoria's vision. Freya's voice filled her thoughts. *Your pledge is witnessed. Now run. Find your pack and run.*

Blinking until her vision restored, she took a faltering step and then another. When she could see again, she broke into a gallop, giving free reign to her wolf. Her goddess commanded her, so she ran.

Revenge remained in her heart. Victoria no longer believed in justice, whether she was sworn to it or not.

I HOPE you enjoyed Valkyrie's Vengeance. Reviews are always appreciated! Don't forget to *join my newsletter* for free reads, exclusive sneak peeks, and giveaways. And please check out Hunger Moon, the next book in the Loki's Wolves series.

ABOUT THE AUTHOR

Melissa Snark is a fantasy and romance author with a particular interest in pirates, werewolves, and mythology. Her Loki's Wolves series combines elements of both in a contemporary fantasy setting. She lives in Northern California with her husband, three children and a glaring of cats.

Join Melissa Snark's newsletter to be notified of new releases.

For more information...
www.melissasnark.com
melissasnark@melissasnark.com

That Old Black Magic Universe

Heart's Desired Mate Series

Love is the Law

A Novel of the Fallen Angels

Prophecy

Aries Cursed series

(A Zodiac Shifters Book)

Ram Rugged by Melissa Thomas

The Bonded (short story) in Crimson Kisses anthology

How to Tame Your Dragon Mate series

(A Zodiac Shifters Book)

Bewitched Dragon Mates by Melissa Thomas